Tales M
and Mysterious

By Enjoy!

Allan Martin

Allan Martin

TP

ThunderPoint Publishing Ltd.

First Published in Great Britain in 2022 by
ThunderPoint Publishing Limited
Summit House
4-5 Mitchell Street
Edinburgh
Scotland EH6 7BD

ISBN: 978-1-910946-88-6 (Paperback)
ISBN: 978-1-910946-89-3 (eBook)
Printed and bound in Great Britain by Clays Ltd, Elcograf S.p.A

www.thunderpoint.scot

Acknowledgements

Most of the stories in this book first appeared in *iScot* magazine. I would like to thank editor Ken McDonald for accepting one story and then encouraging more. I am also grateful to Huw and Seonaid at ThunderPoint for bringing these tales to a wider audience.

Dedication

To Vivien: muse, first reader, fearless critic, sharp-sighted editor.

Contents

The Best and Worst of Times

The Rise and Rise of Carlotta Morazov

Kevin Gramble was a writer. After graduating with a BA in Journalism from the University of Mid-Scotland he'd got a job with the *Wick Advertiser*. After a couple of years he moved to the *Fifeman*. It was somebody there who told him to get out of newspapers: "Most people get their news on TV or the internet. They only buy papers for the puzzles or the celebrity gossip. That's why the papers don't bother with news any more. What there is, they just copy from elsewhere or make up. Special interest mags is the way forward." So Kevin became deputy editor of the monthly *World of Rodents*. He learned a great deal about furry creatures large and small, so much so that four years later he was easily the prime candidate for the editorship of *Pest Exterminator*. Now he was at the top of the tree, but it wasn't enough. He knew he could write, and he needed money. A comfortable flat by the Dundee waterfront just wasn't enough.

He decided to write novels. Visits to bookshops and his local library told him soon enough that crime fiction was what sold. He read enough to get a feel for what seemed to be successful, and then developed his formula. There must be a detective who is dedicated, brutal, flawed and successful, though disliked by his superiors. He must work with a partner who is a complete contrast to him. The cases he deals with must involve frequent killings of a most gruesome type. And only because of his prescient gut feelings, his imaginative leaps, and his dogged persistence after all his colleagues have given up, are the cases solved after a tense final confrontation with the killer. And so Judd Moloch was born.

Inspector Judd Moloch. He'd been a soldier, a junior officer in Afghanistan. Succeeded where others failed because of his willingness to take any measures necessary to succeed. He could when he wanted be brutally destructive: breaking limbs was an easy matter for a big man with a baseball bat. But torture which left no mark was also his metier: with a simple darning needle he could inflict so much pain that a confession was inevitable. Indeed, his confession rate among suspected insurgents was second to none. And he enjoyed being judge, jury and, especially, executioner. The senior officers, in public, disapproved of his methods, but could not argue against their effectiveness. And when a young colonel, vaguely related to the royal family, slapped him on the back, remarking, "That's the spirit, old chap, got to show them who's the boss, eh?" he knew he was untouchable. Of course, they say pride always comes before a fall, and after the summary execution of the mayor and council of a small town in Helmand province, his presence was felt to be embarrassing. He was persuaded to resign, with the promise that, "Don't worry, old chap, you'll see, something will pop up." And indeed, no sooner was he back in the UK than he was offered a job in the Metropolitan Police.

There was no point in writing about Moloch as a lowly PC, so he had him fast-tracked, due to his army background, to detective sergeant. Then, after a particularly difficult case in which a suspected rapist phoned the police to confess after both his kneecaps had been smashed by a man in a balaclava wielding an iron bar, Moloch was transferred to Police Scotland and promoted to Detective Inspector. Kevin recognised that putting his hero in places familiar to his readers would sell more books. Planting his cop in Fiji or Tangier would involve a lot of research that would get in the way of the writing.

This is where the first book would start. Moloch is sent to prove himself to a small town on the edge of the central belt, a depressed place with high unemployment and plenty of crime. He finds most of it is connected to a local gangster, Tam Straikenshaw. By cleverly planting rumours, Moloch sets off a war amongst Straikenshaw's chief henchmen, so that sections of the gang start fighting each other. Kevin got that idea from Dashiell Hammett's *Red Harvest.* When the gang is thus weakened, Moloch then picks off the weaker members, forcing confessions which incriminate those higher up, and eliminating those who won't co-operate. The gangster's corrupt lawyer causes a lot of trouble for Moloch, until he is mysteriously drowned in a sewer. After that, Straikenshaw's ability to defy Moloch is significantly weakened, and the inspector sets up a confrontation, at the end of which the gangster pulls out what could be a weapon and is gunned down by police marksmen. Moloch ensures that a suitable weapon is found in his hand. He then intimidates the remaining gang members until they flee to safer places. The town has been cleaned up, and even if Moloch seems to overdo it at times, law and order has triumphed, and his colleagues stand and applaud as he comes into the divisional HQ to request another assignment.

One problem that emerged as he wrote was that of the sidekick. Kevin found it hard to develop a detective sergeant who would be a strong contrast to Moloch. The DI despises anyone who isn't able to stand up to him and ignores anyone who is. He just doesn't do sharing. However, he doesn't consider women or disabled people to be equals, so the sidekick became wheelchair-bound DS Liala Omala, crippled as a result of Moloch's careless driving whilst chasing a stolen car. She's an IT whizz with a sharp brain and a good imagination, and enough bitterness to vent her spleen on Moloch every time she encounters him. In each book Kevin thought Liala might attempt in a different way to destroy Moloch: in the first book a voodoo curse, in the second, poisoning his coffee, in the third, tipping off his movements to criminals, and so on. Each attempt is of course unsuccessful, but leaves its mark on Moloch, who would become more disturbed and violent as the series developed.

Kevin showed the first draft of *Moloch's Order* to a number of contacts he knew in the publishing world, and soon an ambitious young agent, Salomé O'Brien, took him on. She had a good look at the book and recommended a rewrite, increasing the level of explicit violence, and adding some gratuitous sex. Kevin duly obliged, and a scene where Moloch seduces the gangster's daughter, then beats her up as a warning to him was particularly appreciated. However, Salomé felt that his name would not help him. Kevin Gramble just didn't have the sense of menace which should be appropriate to a writer of gritty crime fiction. Plus he was male. The most successful crime writers, she believed, were female, and she therefore recommended a female *nom de plume*. Thus was born Carlotta Morazov. Kevin agreed that he wouldn't reveal to anyone that he was Carlotta Morazov, at least until they saw how the book was doing.

It was published by Locust Books, a small publisher of crime novels, and was an instant success. Moloch's moral ambiguity attracted the critics, who were able to pontificate about law, order, justice, and human values till the cows came home. The reading public were attracted more by the sex, violence, and ultimate triumph of the good guys. Most readers agreed that the end justified the means. O'Brien Associates now rejected Locust's offer to publish the next Moloch, and secured Kevin a four-book deal with ZOD, a major international publisher, who handed him a £50,000 advance. Now he could bid farewell to *Pest Exterminator* and be his own man. The first thing he bought himself was a car: low-slung, soft-topped, powerful, the sort of car Judd Moloch might drive.

He'd already written the second Moloch book, in which the inspector cleans up a gang of people smugglers supplying slave labour to the fruit farms of south Angus. His new editor, Cara Smythe-Tomkins, however, soon curtly informed him that it was totally unsatisfactory. "Lets face it, Kev," she said during their Zoom conference, "any local writer could churn out this sort of stuff. Locust might drool at it, but we're not so easily impressed. We hired you because you can write, and because Moloch's a great character, not for this. Nobody's interested in people smugglers, or the fruit industry, or places they've not heard of. Or anything that happens in Scotland. You need to think bigger, Kev. What people want now is something that'll give them a bit of a shiver. Think serial killer, the more crazed the better. Think weird violence. Evisceration. Splayed out guts. And something personal to Moloch. Give him a loved one, then kill her off. Get on it, Kev. Earn your keep!"

The result was *Moloch's Watch*, in which Moloch, now based in Manchester, hunts down a serial killer who removes his victims' eyes and mails them to their nearest and dearest. His final victim is Moloch's wife, an attractive nurse whom he has recently married. Moloch's revenge when he finally confronts the killer is a relentless destruction with a club hammer of the man's limbs, one bone-crushing blow for each victim. The final blow, for Moloch's wife, is however not the end, and the final sequence in which the man is disembowelled, following which Moloch tears his heart out with his bare hands, occupied eight pages.

This one was a best-seller throughout the English-speaking world, especially in the USA, and was then translated into all the major world languages. Many readers admitted to having vomited whilst reading the final chapter. Kevin netted another £50,000 and plenty more. Carlotta Morazov had arrived.

However, her fame brought problems. One was an avalanche of letters, emails, tweets, and communications by every possible means, directed to Carlotta via her publishers. There were many offers of marriage, or simply sex, along with a smaller number of complaints about the unnecessary violence in her novels. And even a couple of messages from men who claimed to have emulated Moloch's violent activities. Police found most of these claims to be false, but one claimant, who turned out to be a Detroit police officer, was arrested.

The other problem was the many demands for information about Carlotta herself, and requests for her to appear at book festivals throughout the world. *Moloch's Watch* was shortlisted for a major international book prize, although in the end the award went to Naomi van Schöörach's *My World is Air and Smells of Lemon.* Cara Smythe-Tomkins had been at the ceremony, ready to accept the prize on Carlotta's behalf. The next week she summoned Kevin to a meeting at the publisher's headquarters in London.

He was shown into a high-speed lift on the ground floor of a skyscraper, and came out into an office on the top floor. Cara was waiting, and he was surprised to see Salomé there too. Cara was wearing a grey suit with a short skirt, and Kevin let his eyes caress her thighs as he lowered himself into the deep armchair and sat facing her. She brushed a lock of long auburn hair away from her face.

"Kevin," she said quietly, "Carlotta has arrived. We need to decide what to do with her. Salomé and I have just been having a chat about it, and we're both happy about the way it's going to work out."

"I'm ready too," said Kevin. "I realise, now that the books are so successful, that I'll have to reveal that I'm Carlotta. We could make a big event of it. Disclose my identity right at the end. Or – "

"No, Kevin," whispered Cara, leaning provocatively towards him. "It's not going to be like that."

"Ah, you've already got the revelation event worked out?"

"There isn't going to be a revelation."

"I – I don't understand. People want to see Carlotta Morazov in person."

"And so they will, Kevin. It just won't be you."

"But I'm Carlotta Morazov."

"No, Kevin," put in Salomé. "Remember, Carlotta is an author I invented for you. And I've done a deal with ZOD. On your behalf, of course. It's a good one, a very good one."

"And," Cara continued, "we own her now, not you. In fact, we've already hired a B-list actress based in South Africa who'll play the part of Carlotta Morazov. She's a clever girl and can carry it off well enough. We'll provide her with a good back story and write her speeches."

"Speeches?"

"Yes. The next Moloch book will win a couple of major prizes – we've already set that up."

"But how can you do that? There's competition."

"One of them we sponsor, so we appoint the judges; we simply put in people who do what we tell them. The other was a bit trickier – but the money always gets through in the end."

"But you still need me to write the books."

She laid her hand on his right knee and squeezed it. "Actually, Kevin, we don't. You think you're the only guy who can write this sort of shit? We've already lined up a couple of people who'll write the stuff if necessary."

"What do you mean? This is ridiculous. I've got a contract to write three more books for you."

"Of course you have, darling. Just write them and send them in on time. If they're not good enough, or the plot doesn't fit, our guys can work on them."

"What do you mean, if the plot doesn't fit? I'm the author."

"Poor Kevin. You really don't understand. Moloch isn't just a character from fiction. He's a brand, a product. Our concept designers and promotional engineers have developed a product definition that will maximise our profits from Moloch. Believe me, Kevin, Moloch will just get nastier and nastier. And bigger and bigger. After the books, there will be the films. And the 3D immersion games. And the products. We've already got a deal with a cutlery manufacturer in South Korea for a Moloch knife range. So you see how important it is that we get the books right, don't you?"

"You can't do this to me!" gasped Kevin. "I created Judd Moloch. He's mine, and I'll keep him. Believe me, you haven't heard the end of this." He attempted to jump up from the chair to emphasise the point, but it was so deep and soft that he only got half way up before sinking back into it.

Cara came over to him, perched herself on the arm of his chair, allowing her skirt to ride even further up her thigh, and stroked his cheek with her fingers. "Of course you created him, darling. We're not pushing you out, Kev, of course not. We're just making the most of your creation. In fact, we're so confident in what you're giving us that we'll give you an advance of £100,000 on the next book. *Moloch's Anger* would be a good title. Nice and evocative. It needs to be good. Remember that it's going to win prizes, so throw in a few longer words."

Her words, and especially the money, mollified Kevin, and he left the meeting smiling to himself. His angry outburst had been useful, netted him a bigger advance. Now he'd be closer to the centre of their plans. No-one would take Judd Moloch from him.

Later that afternoon, Cara made a phone call, to someone who knew a man who could fix things. Two weeks later an obscure journalist, until recently the editor of *Pest Exterminator*, was involved in a road accident. It happened at night, on a country road near Brechin on a tight corner, wet with recent rain. The car skidded off the road, hit a tree, burst into flames. There were no witnesses, and no survivors. No-one remembered the man sitting in the pub with Kevin, slipping something into his Pepsi when he went to the toilet.

One person remembered the expensive sports car leaving the pub car park. No-one noticed the more ordinary vehicle following him out of the pub car park. The autopsy on the charred corpse showed traces of alcohol. The police closed the case; another idiot having a drink before jumping into a car that was too powerful for him.

No-one remembered Kevin Gramble. Only a couple of neighbours turned up for his funeral at the local crematorium. Later that week, at the Frankfurt Book Fair, Carlotta Morazov appeared in public for the very first time. Tall, well-rounded, long black hair, fantastic in an evening dress, and gave a great speech too. Her agent, Salomé O'Brien, and her editor, Cara Smythe-Tomkins, received plaudits from the publishing industry for their discovery and nurturing of such a fantastic talent.

The Legend of Archie McLeath

An ordinary evening for Archie McLeath; it gets quieter when you're old. Two boxes of Micro Chips, a 4-in-1 TexMex dip assortment, a four-pack of Tennents Lager, a bottle of cheap vodka, all from Mr Khan's shop, and a DVD. The DVD was called *Bunga-Bunga.* Archie didn't know what that meant, but the man at the stall in the Barras market said it was a good one. The fuzzy photocopied cover seemed to show a cluster of naked bodies. The writing on the back was in a foreign language. The man said the dialogue was in Italian, but he shouldn't worry about that, there was no plot anyway. A bargain at just a pound. And he'd never had cause to complain before about the stallholder's recommendations.

He'd just set up the DVD player, taken one of the boxes of Micro Chips out of the microwave, put it on the coffee table along with the dips, poured a glass of beer and half a tumbler of vodka, when the doorbell rang.

"Shite!" said Archie. He thought about ignoring it, but realised the light would be visible through the faded curtains. That was the disadvantage of living at ground level, in a terrace of cheap houses built first for workers at Scartoun's long-demolished iron foundry. He got up from his old armchair, took a quick slug of vodka to get his limbs moving, and headed for his tiny hallway. From there the front door opened straight onto the street.

Faces of children in the dark drizzle. "Trick or treat, mister?"

Fucking guisers. Fucking Hallowe'en. Should have kept the door shut.

"None of this trick or treat stuff," he growled at them. "If you're proper guisers you'll do a wee song or a poem or a turn of some sort. Let's see it and I'll think about giving yous an orange." He didn't have any oranges, but he'd worry about that when he got to it.

"Fuck off, mister, we're no daein that. This is trick or treat. Just gie us a few quid or we'll soak you." He reckoned the speaker to be about twelve. There were another three or four. One was pointing one of those big plastic water-squirting guns, with a big reservoir on top.

"Piss off, ya pests, I'm no just haundin out money!" Archie was just shuffling round in the narrow hall to shut his door, when another voice cut in.

"Hey you, ya old git, did you no hear what my wee brother just said?" A youth, maybe sixteen, thin, dressed in hoody and jogging pants, at the back of the gang.

"Aye, ah heard, an you're no huvin anything. In ma day guisers was guisers. Now piss off!"

Before he could shut the door, the youth was right in front of him, a foot in his door and a knife in his hand. "Gie my wee brother a tenner, or I'll slice yer neb fur ye!"

Time for a strategic climbdown. "All right, all right, ah'll get yous something."

He shuffled down the hall and into the living room. Took another swig of vodka, to calm down. He was boiling. Threatened by an acned kid who thought he was big just because he'd taken a knife from his mammy's kitchen. Caught sight of the DVD shelf in the corner by the door. An idea. He groped behind the DVDs, felt the cold metal, gently lifted out the sawn-off shotgun. There since Boney Huggin had left it for safe-keeping a year ago. No weapon in Boney's place when the cops raided it the next week, saved him a much longer sentence. This would scare the wee nyaff all right.

He kept the gun behind him and swung it up as he approached the front door again. "All right yous, now aff!"

"Fuck off, grandad," said the youth. "So you've got an old shooter. Put it down before you hurt yerself, ya old plonker!"

It was more of a gut reaction that made Archie pull the trigger. He hadn't even realised the gun was loaded. The blast deafened him and the recoil sent him staggering back until he hit his parents' old hallstand.

When he got back to the door, the youth was lying on his back on the damp street, a big red splodge on his chest. The three younger boys stared down at him.

"He's fucking killed my brother!" screamed the one who'd come to his door. "Hey, ya bastard, you know who my da is? Candie McKane, that's who. An he'll be back to cut your fucking heid aff." With that the three boys ran off.

Archie contemplated the corpse lying in the empty street. In a respectable neighbourhood folks would be leaning out their windows to see what was going on. But this wasn't that kind of place. It was the kind of place where nobody noticed. He shut the front door.

He'd killed a kid. Even if he was a ned, that was bad news. But Candie McKane's. That was worse than bad news. McKane was Frank Glaister's number two. And Frank Glaister ruled this one-horse town straddling the road to England as if he was the Emperor of China.

He had only one option, and not much time. He reached behind the DVDs again and pulled out the box of shotgun cartridges, put them in a plastic bag. Then added the automatic and the other box of ammo that Boney had left. Then added the bottle of vodka. Put his jacket on. Went through the kitchen to the back door and out. Shut the door on his life in Scartoun.

His old Astra was parked in the back lane. He'd got it for £300 from Jamie Hanson's garage. He knew it was stolen, the plates were fake, but that saved him paying the road tax. As long as you drove carefully, nobody bothered about an old Astra.

He set off down the lane, then turned right into Wallace Street. Thin persistent rain, and nobody about. Fifty yards down he could see the bus shelter across the road. There were two people waiting, an old man with a walking stick and a flat cap, and that old witch from two doors down. Always scowling at him. Complained to the council about his back garden. What was she doing peering into it anyway?

He stopped the car, pointed the shotgun out the window, and blasted it at the shelter. With a jangling crash, the glass shattered. The old hag ran off, but tripped on something and fell in a puddle. The old man just stood looking at him. Then he spat into the street and went over to help the old woman.

Archie felt ashamed. That was nothing to be proud of, the sort of stuff kids would do. He had to be better than that.

He drove on, took another swig. Shit, the bottle was empty. Further along Wallace Street was Mr Khan's shop, he'd get some more there. Mr Khan opened till late.

He pulled up outside the shop, and went in. Behind the counter a thin man with a badly shaved head held a knife to Mr Khan's throat. He registered Archie's arrival. "Piss off, the shop's shut. Get me?"

"Aye, no problem, pal," said Archie. He glanced at Mr Khan, and knew the shopkeeper would die rather than hand over a penny. He knew the other man, too. Skinny Laidlaw. He was probably high on whatever shit he could find. But that wasn't right. Not Mr Khan's shop. He turned and left.

Back at the car, he took the automatic from the bag and went back into the shop.

"Ah told ye tae…"

Archie put two bullets into Skinny's chest before he could finish the sentence. The old skills came back so easily. Skinny slumped out of sight behind the counter without a word.

Mr Khan looked down at the body. "A sad character," he said. "Thank you, Mr McLeath. No need to worry about Mr Laidlaw, my sons will help me get rid of him later. Can I get you something?"

"I was just wanting a bottle of vodka. The cheap stuff."

Mr Khan turned to reach up to the row of Russky brand vodka bottles behind him. Then he paused, and leaned further down the shelves, selected a bottle and handed it to Archie. The bottle had a green label with a buffalo on it, and there was a blade of grass inside it.

"A wee thank you, Mr McLeath. On the house. The best there is. Or so I'm told." He smiled.

"Is it American, then?" asked Archie. "I mean, yon buffalo."

"No, no, it's Polish. That's a bison. The grass is what they eat. But it's good stuff. Absolutely the best. Very strong, so take care. Now, I'd better shut the shop a little early."

Back to the car. He felt better. Done something to make the world a nicer place. Nobody would miss Skinny Laidlaw. And the vodka tasted good. Strong, anyway.

What to do next. He didn't have long before Scartoun wouldn't treat him with amiable indifference any longer. He needed to run. Maybe hit the A74, get down to England. Someone told him once that Manchester was the place to hide.

There were places there he could disappear. Salford, Burnley, Rochdale, or was it Rotherham, places people here had never heard of.

He drove up Wallace Road until he reached the High Street. The wide thoroughfare in the centre of the town had once hosted markets and cattle sales. Now it offered easy parking and downmarket shops, a chippie and a Chinese. As he glanced up the deserted High Street, his eyes rested on the Ling Wah restaurant. An idea alighted on his damp forehead and crept quietly into his brain. A final act before departure.

He parked outside the pound shop and got out the car. He put the automatic in his pocket along with a few shotgun cartridges. Then he picked up the shotgun, made sure both barrels were loaded, and walked across the cobbled heritage of former prosperity towards the restaurant.

Everybody in Scartoun knew that this was where Frank Glaister ate. Always Frank or Mr Glaister. He remembered the story of one ambitious henchman who'd called him 'Frankie'. Mr Glaister cut his tongue out with a razor, and he was left to bleed to death by the war memorial. At least his death saved him the humiliation of having to mumble for the rest of his life.

He walked in the door. A few paces in, at a table on his left, sat Frank Glaister, bent over a plate of grey-green curry. Frank was big and filled his chair, with more of him to spare. He wore a grey suit and a scarlet tie, and his bald head gleamed. Next to him sat a woman with a large bust and bottle-blonde hair. Archie didn't have time to notice what she was eating.

Frank looked up at Archie. "What the fuck do you want?" he'd said, before he noticed the shotgun. Archie fired one barrel at his chest. Again he underestimated the recoil. Frank was forced back into his seat, his head upright, his face missing. Then he lurched forward again, and his bloody head splattered into the curry sauce. The blonde screamed.

Archie noticed a movement in the far corner of the room. Frank's minders had woken up to what was happening. The two men stood up, groping in pockets for their weapons. Archie fired the second barrel towards a spot between them. Both were caught in the hail of pellets. One fell backwards immediately. The other remained standing, his face pock-marked with blood. He had his pistol in his hand and was waving it in Archie's general direction.

"Tam! My eyes!" he shouted. "I cannae see. Where the fuck is he?" He fired a shot, which hit the ceiling.

Archie put the shotgun on a table and took out the automatic. He shot the man in the chest and he clattered down behind the table.

He walked over towards the table. The other man was on the floor, groaning, and beginning to pull himself up, pistol in hand. Candie McKane.

"You're too old for this, Candie," said Archie. "Time to retire." He shot him in the head.

Looking round the restaurant, he realised the blonde had disappeared. There was no-one else there, except for a Chinese family in the opposite corner, near the door to the kitchen. Father, mother and three children. Bowls of food filled their table.

"Sorry about this," said Archie. "Just yous carry on with yer meal."

As he spoke, he noticed the door to the kitchen move, and something swished through the air towards him. He jerked his head back but felt a sharp sting at the left side. Something clattered on the floor behind him; he looked round to see a small cleaver, and near it the top half of his ear. He felt warm liquid running down his neck and his hand came away bloody from where his ear should have been.

"Fuck's sake!" he grunted. "Ya bastards," and made for the kitchen. As he shoved the door open, he caught a movement, and was able to cover his face with his left hand as hot fat was flung over him. He felt his head and hands burn, and screamed. He fired several shots around the kitchen, and heard a door shut. They'd gone.

He rushed over to sink, turned the cold tap on, and stuck his head under it, held it there for a minute or two, till the pain eased under the chill of the water. He wiped the fat off his head and hands with a towel. This wasn't good.

He came back into the restaurant. Now there was nobody there at all. He was thirsty, needed a drink. He put the pistol back in his pocket, reloaded the shotgun, and laid it on the table. There was a narrow bar next to the kitchen door, a few spirit bottles behind it, and further down a glass-fronted chilled cupboard with bottles in it. He selected the most colourful label. It claimed to be Chinese, but he suspected it was made in Birmingham. Or somewhere like that. He opened the bottle using the opener fastened on the wall, sat down at a table, drank it from the bottle. The lager was cool and wet, it didn't taste of much, but that didn't matter. He finished it.

He felt a lot better after the drink, though his head and hand were still sore. Time to get across the High Street, pick up the car, and hit the road

He'd only taken two or three steps across the cobbles when all at once the night became day. Powerful lights shone from the steps of the old burgh hall. A voice boomed out. "ARMED POLICE! DROP YOUR WEAPON. PUT YOUR HANDS UP! NOW!"

He paused. What to do next. At least he'd achieved something, done a bit of good. He remembered a film from his youth, where two amiable outlaws pulled off a final heist in a town somewhere in South America, then got surrounded by soldiers, with no way out. In the final scene they make a few humorous remarks, then both leap forward out of their hiding place, and into legend.

"The legend of Archie McLeath," he said to himself. "Aye, that's a good one."

"PUT THE GUN DOWN!" boomed the voice. "OR WE FIRE!"

Archie stood up straight, raised the shot gun, and shouted, "Ya fuck..."

Two bullets hit his chest, and one passed through his right eye, taking part of his skull out behind him. Another missed him and shattered the window of the Ling Wah restaurant.

But Archie wasn't part of it any more. Now he was legend.

Dangerous Places

A Place for Inspiration

Finnich Glen. A deep and narrow rift in the gentle undulation of the land. Perpendicular rock walls and at the bottom a burn that only the most determined gorge walkers could negotiate. In Victorian times a steep stone staircase had been set into a crack in the side of the gorge, so that guests could descend the seventy feet to the floor of the glen and immerse themselves in its romantic splendour. Curiously, Finnich Glen, though never quite forgotten, did not become one of those sites to which every visitor to Scotland is pointed. Even now, despite its featuring as a backdrop in film and TV, and its closeness to Glasgow, it still seems off the beaten track. There are no road signs nor dedicated parking, no visitor centre nor café. The only signs warn of the danger of death.

Maybe that's why the members of the South Lennox Ladies' Writing Group were so pleased at the opportunity of a night-time visit. They'd been there the previous summer on their annual outing, during the day of course, and, clinging to the rope tethered at the top of the semi-ruinous staircase, managed to clamber down into the glen to marvel at its romantic potential. The four poets who made up half the group drew into themselves the sights, sounds, smells, and textures which they would distil into verse.

The other four set themselves to peopling the glen with the actors who would drive a short story, even a novel. Kate Drewrigge, as slim and dark-haired at sixty as she had been at forty, well, maybe not quite, pictured a historical scene, a young man of noble extraction, rendered fugitive by his choice of king, fleeing from brutish pursuers, encountering a peasant girl seeking a lost sheep. Amy Carruthers, shorter, round-faced and curly-haired, imagined two women, walking the gorge hand-in-hand, when they find, almost drowned, a strange bearded figure, who speaks only Gaelic and has fallen from another time. Jennifer McCusker, large in a way that Glasgow sometimes sadly makes its women, puffing after the descent, saw a Victorian lady creeping gingerly down the staircase at dusk to meet her lover, unaware of her husband's hateful gaze from above. And Winifred Calman, who made no attempt to hide her sixty-seven years, and wore her grey hair in a pony-tail as she had all her life, conjured a scream from a dark shape falling from the cliff towards the rocks below.

Kate, the secretary of the group, and, two days a week, a hospital administrator, had heard from a junior doctor about the night-time event in the glen. It was very hush-hush, the landowner would no doubt try to stop it. The plan, hatched by a group of young doctors, was to gather after dark one evening in December, and set off fireworks from the floor of the glen. Then they'd repair to the Wayfarer's Inn at Croftamie for drinks, and to get their photos up onto Facebook and Twitter.

The writing group were overjoyed to be let in on the secret, and to be able to visit the glen again, and in such exciting circumstances. The literary output from last year's visit had been disappointing. Judy Gibbon's poem described a tuft of grass half way down the staircase, 'proud and lonely watcher of our all-too-sad endeavours.' Rena McCain's followed a brave and determined salmon on his journey up the glen through the raging water of the burn in spate. Angelina Crawley produced an obscene limerick starting 'I once made a pact with the devil,' which caused some hilarity. And Solveig McKellar had written her poem, as usual, in her native Norwegian, but her hesitant translation made little sense, other than that the verse was about running water.

Kate's historical tale somehow fell flat; perhaps the dialogue was too modern, suggested someone. Amy's narrative built up some tension, but seemed a bit similar to a recent TV series. Jennifer's piece focused, in lengthy physiological detail, on the lovers' passionate embrace; but when asked what happened next, she exclaimed testily that she'd not had time to finish it. Winifred had set her story in the early 1950s: a nurse looks down into the glen and remembers traumatic events during the retreat to Dunkirk, when a soldier had paused to save her, at the cost of his own life. At the end of the story, overcome by her sense of personal loss, and the meaningless stupidity of war, the nurse closes her eyes and, clutching the wristwatch the soldier had given her as a keepsake, steps off the cliff.

It was Winifred's custom, after each meeting, to give printouts of what she'd read to one of the others, and ask for more comments in private. Jennifer had read the Finnich Glen story, and confessed she didn't find it very gripping, and thought the ending rather pointless. Better, she'd said, if the nurse turned away and walked back towards the road, to get on with her life.

It was a few months later when her husband remarked, "Isn't there a Jennifer McCusker in your writing group? I saw her name on a magazine in the paper shop – I had to move it to find my *Meccano Monthly*. I got you a copy." Winifred took the slim and shiny volume of *We Are She* magazine. She'd not heard of it. And there was Jennifer's story. Except that Jennifer called herself 'Jen B. McCusker', and it was Winifred's story. The nurse standing on the cliff remembering the soldier who helps and dies; and in the end the nurse tosses the wristwatch down into the glen and turns back to the path. Winifred could not speak, as a dark pool of hollowness spread inside her. It was as if something had been stolen not just from her head, but from her entire being. A theft of such intimacy that she felt as if her creative self had been abused.

She drew Jennifer aside after the next meeting, said she'd seen the story and asked why she'd copied it. Jennifer shrugged. "You don't know the writing business, do you, Winifred? My story's got a few similarities with yours, but it's a completely different work. Yours is just sentimental. Mine's more thoughtful, deeper. And my ending's truer to the character. Happens all the time - two people have the same idea, develop it differently. Think how often two films with a similar theme appear at the same time. Publishing's like that too. You've just got to take it on the chin."

Winifred wasn't left satisfied. It was her story, all of it, her creative act. But worse was Jennifer's smug justification for her theft. Something would have to be done.

They decided to share cars for this year's trip. Winifred didn't mind driving, and offered to take three others; Kate,

Amy and Solveig immediately volunteered to join her. She was relieved she didn't have Jennifer, whose girth meant she always got the front seat, and Winifred didn't want to listen to her talking about the published writers in whose circle she seemed to move. Jennifer got a place in Rena's car, but a couple of days before the trip, Rena emailed her apologies to the group; she'd gone down with a stomach bug. No-one else offered to take Jennifer. "She'll have to come in her tank now," thought Winifred.

At 7.40 Winifred and her passengers arrived at the junction near the glen, and squeezed alongside the other vehicles already there. It had been raining earlier, but at least that had stopped, though there was cloud overhead and no stars visible. They walked down the road, keeping their torches focused on the narrow path and watching out for traffic, around the corner and over the bridge. They passed a padlocked metal gate in the wall, and a few yards beyond it came to the gap where the barbed wire had been trampled down. The path above the glen was muddy, and they had to tread very carefully. The others were waiting at the head of the staircase. By torchlight the decrepit steps looked wet and slimy. The young doctors, probably all experienced mountaineers, were already at the bottom, torch-beams moving about in the well of darkness. Solveig said she'd go down, and produced a head-torch and an ice-axe. "Anything for a bunch of men," whispered Amy to Winifred.

The others decided to view the display from above. In the light of their torches, the trunks of the spindly trees clinging to the cliff-side marked the lip of the gorge, and the carpet of fallen leaves in front of them showed the edge clearly, so they positioned themselves as near as seemed safe. Winifred noticed Jennifer pushing through to the front to get the best view. She kept herself nearer the rear. The setting was already getting into her head, stories struggling to be born. She let one grow, a tale of secret vengeance, an unforgotten wrong set right by a violent act of justice. It was too dark to jot the outline down in the notebook she always carried with her, but she would not forget it.

At eight the torches were switched off and the display began. Now the group discovered that whilst the rockets were easily visible, the fireworks which didn't rise out of the glen were difficult to see, so a certain amount of movement took place, depending where the next burst of light or sound seemed to come from. One of the young doctors must have brought a big CD player, as they heard the ominous urgency of *The Ride of the Valkyries* rise out of the gorge and vibrate around them as glowing yellow balls sprang up to explode not far above them like shells. Now came a starburst high overhead, and necks craned to see the myriad glittering sparks that whined off in every direction. Winifred felt her story write itself in her mind. This was the creative process, what made her a writer. It was part of her, but she felt part of it too.

Now they saw a deep red glow emanating from the depth of the gorge, and there was more shuffling of positions. A new insight flickered in her head: dared she make the tale real? She saw in front of her Jennifer's bulky outline and moved forward. Now it was pitch dark. Then the eerie red glow again, and vague silhouettes moving hither and thither. Where was Jennifer? Someone bumped into her, she pushed them away. And then, out of the gorge, a hideous scream, suddenly truncated, leaving behind its dissonant echo. A purple blob drifted up into the sky and with a dull pop burst into a billow of burning snowflakes that drifted away on an invisible breeze.

"Oh my God!" cried a voice. Judy's. "Jennifer's gone! Where is she?"

Someone produced a torch and swung it round, pointing at each in turn. All of them, except Jennifer. They noticed the silence – *The Ride of the Valkyries* had stopped in mid-gallop. A rocket whooshed up into the dark sky and exploded with a loud white bang, followed by continuous crackling as tiny lights were born and died in seconds. They could see torch-beams moving below, towards a spot at the foot of the wall, out of sight from those above.

The sound of bamboo xylophones filled the silence, and Kate answered her mobile. "What?...Oh God, no. Are you sure?...What'll we do?...You have? OK, we'll wait here." She switched the phone off as the others looked at her, briefly illuminated by eerie blue light. "It's Jennifer. At the bottom. They, they think she's dead. We've to stay here. That was

Donald below. Ambulance and police are on the way."

"Can't they stop the fireworks?" Amy had to shout as a cacophony of sizzling and fizzing broke out around them.

"No. It's one of those big pre-programmed boxes. You just light the touch paper, and then the whole programme runs. You're not even supposed to go near it once it's started."

The police were there almost immediately. It seemed someone living nearby had already reported the display and complained about the noise. The five left at the top were led by two uniformed officers back to where the cars were parked, now joined by two police vehicles. As they came up they heard the siren of the approaching ambulance. A police car led them in convoy – Angelina with Judy, and Winifred with Amy and Kate – to the police station in Milngavie. They were told to wait in a room.

Each was interviewed in turn by a uniformed sergeant, along with a female officer who said nothing throughout. He took their details, then asked where they'd been, what they'd seen. Winifred apologised, she couldn't help them very much. She hadn't seen Jennifer fall. People had been moving around, confusing shadows.

"Could Ms McCusker have been accidentally jostled by someone in the dark?" asked the sergeant.

"Yes, I suppose that's possible," answered Winifred, "but I didn't see. I wasn't near the edge, I don't like heights. And it was slippy, with the mud. At my age, I have to be careful on my feet."

The sergeant thanked them, said a report would go to the Procurator Fiscal, to decide whether a Fatal Accident Inquiry was needed. "That'll only happen if it's suspicious, so I don't expect you've anything to worry about," he added.

Back home, Winifred tried to calm down. She'd phoned her husband from the police station, and when she got back, a glass of wine awaited her. She swigged it back in one and shivered. Told him what had happened, that Jennifer had slipped and fallen off the cliff. He comforted her, reassured her everything would be OK. "It does sound like an open-and-shut case. I mean, someone her size going near a slippery cliff edge is asking for trouble."

His words were prescient, for it was decided that no inquiry was necessary, and the death was judged accidental. The group would meet again at Jennifer's funeral.

Winifred thought of writing her story down, the one that had come to her in the darkness at the top of the cliff. But it was too close to what had happened. She dared not see it on paper.

She was not a great internet user. She visited a couple of sites about writing and found the advice useful. She noticed on one a comment made by someone called Jen, and remembered that Jennifer had used that name too, in *We As She*. She typed 'Jen B McCusker' into a search engine, and soon she was looking at Jennifer's website, headed 'A Writer's Den.' One of the menu items along the top was 'My Published Work,' and Winifred went straight there. There was a list of titles, with the name of the magazine, the date, and a short summary of the story. Sure enough, there was the one copied from her own, and she felt again the anger that had come on first seeing it in the magazine.

But further down the list she had another surprise. Published in the February edition of *The Lively Quill* magazine was a story of a young Jacobite, son of a clan chief, fleeing from redcoats along the foot of a narrow gorge, when he meets a girl from a nearby village. Surely this was Kate's story. And in the March edition of *Dumbartonshire Woman* was a tale of two women walking in a deep and lonely glen, when they come across the dishevelled and exhausted figure of a bearded man, who had apparently travelled here from the past. Here was Amy's story too! When she looked further, she found a poem very like one of Judy's, and finally, in the *Balloch Advertiser*, a limerick beginning, 'I once made a pact with the Devil.'

Winifred was astounded. Jennifer had been a serial plagiariser. And she hadn't known. Then she thought, what if others had found out, had the same experience with Jennifer as she had? She remembered the shuffling figures on the cliff-top. What had been happening? Was it like *Murder on the Orient Express*? Had they all conspired to push her off? But surely then they'd have brought her into the plot too. Perhaps just one of them, with the same idea as herself, justice for the abuse of creative minds. She recalled the figure who'd bumped into her. She'd thought it might have been Jennifer, but what if it were someone else?

The funeral was at the crematorium at Clydebank. It was raining. There were hardly any mourners, and no family apart from an elderly lady led by a bored carer, who told Winifred, "I brought her over from the home. She doesn't remember who Jennifer is any more. She thinks this is her husband's funeral. He died eighteen years ago."

The writing group sat together in the second row. Winifred's husband had come with her, but he sat further back, so the group could sit together. The service was perfunctory, conducted by an elderly minister who yawned during the hymns. Winifred was surprised to see Kate rise to give a short speech, describing Jennifer as a developing writer, cut off before she could fulfil her full potential, and saying how much the writing group would miss her warm presence and incisive discussions at their meetings.

There was no gathering afterwards to remember the deceased, and as the group members made for their cars, Winifred caught up with Kate, drew her away from her husband, and whispered to her, "I saw her website."

"Yes," said Kate, "a couple of us did. Everything stolen."

"So justice was done."

Kate looked sharply at Winifred, then smiled. "Yes," she said, "you could look at it that way. You know, Winifred, that night, in the dark, I had a great idea for a story. But I daren't write it now."

Incident at Dunagoil

We often visit the Isle of Bute; it's easy to get there and back in a day from our home in Greenock, and since the introduction of Road Equivalent Tariff the ferry prices are more affordable, especially as there are now just the two of us again. Dunagoil is one of our favourite places on the island. It's a ridge-like outcrop on the island's west coast, and, as the name suggests, there was an iron-age fort there. You can still recognise bits of the stone walls. We park the car in the layby on the single track road that runs down to the old monastery site at Kingarth, and walk down a track between two big fields to the gate in the wall at the end. The narrow path that gets you to the summit is near the south end of the ridge on its eastern flank. Once on top, you can see up and down the coast of Bute, but especially fine is the view across to Arran. We bring a picnic and eat it sitting near the cliff at the northern end where we can see the sun gilding the water below and beyond it the cloud hanging over the peaks that form the Sleeping Warrior. As the seasons change, so does the view, from Alpine snowscape through rain-girt gloom to the jagged profile rising sun-warmed from the heat haze.

This was a spring day, a Friday I think, sunny but cool, a light breeze from the south-west hinting that cloud might be on the way. That day I'd made the sandwiches – smoked salmon, egg mayonnaise and rocket – and we were just finishing off with a choc chip muffin when we noticed the family below, on the shore below the cliffs. Two adults, he in a red and she in a green waterproof jacket, a youth in a black jacket and jeans, and a dog, a small brown one. As we watched, Anne said to me, "Look, the parents aren't speaking to each other; they've had an argument about something." I hadn't noticed – I'm a man, after all, we're not good at noticing things like that – but when I did focus my attention on them, it was clear. Each of the three adults moved alone, walking apart from the other two, while the dog ran about between them.

As I watched the man drew close to the woman – they were clearly talking but I couldn't hear what was being said. The son stood a little way off, watching them. All of a sudden the man hit the woman, slapped her hard across the face so that she staggered back a few steps. The son hurried over to her and put an arm round her, looking at the man as if daring him to come on. But the father turned away began to walk around the rock pools as if the others did not exist. He picked up a stick and threw it for the dog to chase.

"No-one has the right to behave like that," said Anne. "We should do something about it. Report it to the police or something."

"That could be difficult," I said. "We don't know who they are. And we don't know whether the wife would welcome the police being brought into it."

"If he does that again, we should certainly report it. We could follow them back to the car and get the number. Then it could be passed on the authorities where they live. Maybe Social Services already know of them."

We busied ourselves with packing up. Then we clambered back down the path. Back on the low ground again, however, Anne suggested we go up Little Dunagoil. That's a kind of junior version, a smaller echo of Dunagoil, a ridgelet lying to the east of the main one. We went straight up the steep grassy side, my rucksack lighter than before lunch, and soon stood at the top. Little Dunagoil had been fortified too, and the line of a rampart was visible under the turf. The day was still clear, although clouds were beginning to form in the west. Looking towards the road, we could see the gate in the wall, and the track that led up to the road. The big field to the right of the track had something starting to grow in it, a bright green frosting on its brown surface. The field to the left extended from the track down to a little bay; it had cows in it, amongst them a few calves. The cows were spread out across the field, some had even made their way down to the beach and were standing on the sand. I wondered whether they ate seaweed.

Then we saw the family, presumably on the way back to their car. This time the son and his mother walked ahead, and the man lagged some distance behind, occasionally picking up stones and throwing them aimlessly into the sea. The dog rushed into the water after each one, stood in the shallows, then returned without success to await the next cast. It was an odd sort of beast, maybe part pit bull and part West Highland terrier, an odd mixture. Perhaps that would make for a more excitable or aggressive animal. I don't know anything about dogs.

After one angry-looking throw, the man looked towards the woman. "Bitch!" he shouted. "You bloody bitch! Why don't you just clear off. We don't need you. Do we, son?"

The woman paused. Was she going to respond? Then the son put his arm round her again, and was talking quietly to her. They moved on, ignoring the man, came to the gate in the wall, and passed through onto the muddy track between the two fields, heading up to the gate at the roadside.

The man continued throwing stones into the sea, and we could hear him muttering to himself, though the words were unclear. We watched the dog rushing into the shallow water, yelping furiously, then dashing back again. Eventually the man drifted off towards the gate in the wall, and opened it for the dog to bound through onto the track before following.

The dog soon caught sight of the cows in the field on the left, and started barking at them.

"He needs to get that dog under control," said Anne. "Those cows aren't going to like it."

The woman and the youth had almost reached the road now, and paused, I supposed at the sound of the barking, to look back. Beyond them, in the layby, the only car other than ours was one of those big grey tanks. I supposed it was theirs. The woman shouted back to the man, "Get him on the lead, Geoff. He might start chasing the cows."

"Piss off!" shouted the man. "Let the bugger enjoy himself for once." Then he turned to the dog. "Go on, Buster, you show those women who's the boss." The dog ran up to the wire mesh fence, yapping again, and the man shouted, this time at the cows, "You think you're having good time, eh? All that grass, eh? Well, just remember, stupid cows, that I'll be eating you one day. Go on, clear off!" He laughed as the dog intensified its efforts, jumping up at the fence.

But the cows didn't clear off. Cows aren't like sheep. Sheep run when dogs come; the ancestral memory of the wolf. But cows are bigger and heavier; when they're under attack, they bunch together. If there's a lion after them, they might run. But a dog, no way. The cows near the fence seemed to be attracted by the barking, and others began to lumber over from further off. Soon there were maybe two dozen of them leaning over the fence, staring at the dog, and others coming up from behind. They didn't dissuade the dog, which barked even more furiously.

The fence was topped by barbed wire. I'd once asked a farmer why all his fields were surrounded by barbed wire. Was it to keep walkers out? No, he'd said, it's the only thing that'll stop the cows pushing the fence over. Short of a stone wall, they've enough weight to push most fences over. But they don't like the barbed wire. Mind you, he added, if it keeps walkers out too, that's OK with me.

Then I noticed a cow coming through the fence onto the track. I hadn't even noticed there was a gate there. Someone must have left it open. More cows ambled through the gateway, blocking the track, then filling it as more filed through and made their way unhurriedly towards the dog and the man. "This is not good," said Anne. "We'd better get down there." We began to make our way down the easier slope on the side facing the track.

I could still see them. The man waved his arms at the advancing herd. "Hey, get back to your bloody field!" he shouted. It had no effect. "Buster," he yelled, "see those buggers off, will you?" The dog ran at the approaching cows, barking and jumping at them. They plodded on and the dog disappeared amongst them. Then the barking stopped.

"Buster, where the fuck are you?" shouted the man. "You bastards! Get out my bloody way!" He tried to push through the crowd of beasts, milling slowly around. He got in amongst them, shouting for the dog. Then he seemed to get stuck between two of the cows, and then sank out of sight. The cows moved casually about.

As we reached the flatter ground in front of the gate in the wall, we could see the lumbering crowd began to disperse. The threat had been dealt with. One made its way back through the gateway into the field, the others drifted after. Even before the last one had gone, I was at the gate in the wall, while Anne had her phone out to call emergency services.

When I got through the gate onto the track I could see that it was too late for anything. The dog was no more than a darker patch in the trampled mud. The man was more recognisable, by the occasional glimpses of the red top and blue denims. His head was a reddish patch of blood, brain and mud, with white fragments of bone here and there. The rest of him was as crushed as a herd of cows could manage. It was as if he had been flattened out and then carefully blended into the consistency of the mud.

At the top of the track, the woman and the boy stood as if transfixed. Anne hurried past me on up to them, put her arms round them, partly to comfort, partly to keep them from coming back. Meanwhile I shooed the last lingering bovine back through the gate into the field, and shut it, which required hitching a loop of thick wire over the gatepost, no easy task as it was necessary to lift the gate at the same time.

When I finally reached the mother and son, they still seemed dazed. "That dog were always a bad un," said the woman. "He were always going to end up summat like this." A North of England accent. We stayed with them till the ambulance and the police arrived.

Later on, as we sat on the ferry back to Wemyss Bay, Anne said to me, "The gate into the field was shut when we walked down. I'm sure of it. Who could have opened it?"

"The farmer?" I suggested.

"No. We'd have seen all the cows moving towards him if he'd turned up. And farmers aren't that careless. Cows are money to them."

"Another walker?"

"But we didn't see anyone. And there weren't any other cars in the layby."

"What are you thinking, Anne?"

"What if she opened it herself, as she passed?"

"It wouldn't have been that easy. You have to hold the gate up while you flip the wire over the gatepost."

"Maybe the son helped."

"But she told the man to keep the dog on the lead."

"Perhaps she knew just how he would react."

"Should we tell the police?"

"Tell them what?" said Anne. "We didn't see the gate being opened. And we weren't watching it all the time, so it's quite possible somebody else nipped down and opened it. It's not likely, but it's possible. All we have is a suspicion."

Out of the Rain

One night it rained. A night in March, and the rain fell, as winter's grip relaxed. Out in the dark, dulled by the sound and the substance of the rain, a car door slammed, a vehicle drove off. Inside, in the warm living room of a cottage on the edge of a town somewhere to the North of Dundee, a grandfather clock with ponderous chimes struck ten. Across the room, in a pool of light under an old-fashioned standard lamp, Philip Learmonth sat in his leather armchair. He was reading *The History of Reading* by Alberto Manguel. You may think it odd that he waited until his retirement as a librarian to read about the history of reading, but he had until then been satisfied with the history of alphabets and of languages, which he had studied as a student. He had assumed the importance, the essence, was in the signs and the sounds, overlooking what now seemed obvious, that the fundamental fact about reading is the creation of meaning. It is not the words, but what we make of them.

The clock's chimes were a comfort to him, a reminder of the regularity of things, and as the last one died away he was about to turn again to his book, when he was shaken out of his comfortable state of being by the ringing of his doorbell. He frowned at the irritating and incessant buzzing – the button by his front door had a tendency to stick – put the book down by his evening glass of whisky – a 14-year-old Oban – and eased himself out of the chair. Reaching the hallway, he switched on the light which would illuminate the front steps, checked the security chain was in place, then opened the door a fraction.

As the outside air invaded the hall, he heard the heavy whisper of the falling rain on the lawn and felt the fingers of dampness exploring his face.

There was a woman there. It was difficult to tell what she looked like, because she wore a raincoat with a shiny black finish across which streams of water were running, and one of those shapeless hats that men wear to go fishing. She was shorter than he was, not slim, not fat. She leaned forward eagerly, and he noticed thick glasses on a plump white face.

“Darren,” she said. “For heaven’s sake, let me in! I’m soaked through.” When he hesitated, she went on, “Darren, can’t we sort this out inside? Please.” The voice was a little hoarse but not unpleasant, he thought it might be Fife rather than Dundee or Angus, and it told him she was no longer a girl.

“I’m sorry,” he said, “I’m afraid there’s some mistake. No-one called Darren lives here. Perhaps you have the wrong house. This one is called Auster Cottage. Which house were you looking for?”

“The house is right,” she insisted, “It’s not a house I can forget. The laburnum tree in the middle of the lawn. Nothing’s changed. Doesn’t Darren live here any more? I’ve come so far. Do you know where he is?”

Was it her standing there in the rain, was it her voice, puzzled rather than pleading, or something inside himself, that made Philip Learmonth open the door, and beckon her in, out of the rain and the dark, into his house.

The damp air and the smell of wet earth came in with her, filled the little hallway as she stood on the rug dripping.

“Let me take your coat and hat,” Philip offered, and she took them off and passed them to him. He could see now she was wearing a shapeless brown fleece, jeans which were rather wet below the knees, and black trainers. Her hair was dark and shoulder-length and framed her face. Behind the thick lenses her eyes seemed enormous.

“I’ll take off my shoes,” she said, “They’re a bit muddy.” She sat on the old upright chair which Philip had inherited from his parents, and took them off, placing then neatly under the chair. Philip admired this sign of tidiness. As a librarian he valued organisation. She smiled. She had a winning smile, he thought.

“Would you like a cup of tea or coffee?” he asked.

“Tea would be fine, thanks. Milk, no sugar. Shall I…” She gestured with her hand towards the living room doorway.

“Yes, of course. Please, make yourself at home.”

When he came back with the tea, she was sitting in the leather armchair, with her legs curled up beneath her. “This used to be my favourite place,” she said. “And you’ve had a stove put in. Darren was thinking about one, but he never got round to it. It's lovely. I can watch the flames for hours."

"I'm Philip Learmonth," said Philip. "I'm a librarian. That is, I was, till I retired. I bought this place then, that was about six months ago. It came with much of the furniture included."

"Yes, I can see that," she said. "I'm Judy. I used to live here, with Darren. I guess he's not here now."

"No," said Philip, "Dare I ask what happened?" He surprised himself. He would not normally ask such a question. Did she invite it?

"It wasn't good. I think he wanted someone younger. I left, maybe eight months ago. I've been in Australia, I didn't realise Darren had moved out, I thought he would still be here. I was hoping to make things up again."

"Why did you come back? From Australia, I mean."

"It didn't work out. I had nowhere else to go."

"Where did you leave your car?" asked Philip. He suspected this was the wrong question, he'd heard the car drive off, but couldn't think how else to ask it.

"Oh, I don't have a car, I came in a taxi. Once I've dried out a bit I'll call another. There must be a B and B in town."

"Oh no, I can't just chuck you out," Philip heard himself say, "Really. Look, why don't you sleep in the spare room? In the morning you can work out where you want to go next."

"That's very kind of you, Philip." Yes, she had a winning smile.

When Philip woke up next morning he smelt fresh coffee and toast. In the kitchen, Judy was sitting at the table, drinking coffee. He made some toast for himself. The coffee was fresh and strong. It felt good that someone else had made it.

"So little has changed," said Judy, "only Darren didn't have so many books. He had DVDs instead. He must have left a lot of his furniture."

"Yes, I moved from a small flat in Edinburgh, so I didn't have much. Apart from the books, of course."

"Did you meet him then, when you were buying the place?"

"No, it was a bank that was selling it. A repossession, they said."

"Ah. I guess he didn't keep up the payments. I helped him there. I had a little business, dog walking and grooming."

"Out here?"

"No, in Dundee. But I sold the car to get to Australia. Perth. Do you know it?"

"No, I've never been there."

"It's hot and dry, and the earth is red. And there are kangaroos. I don't mean in the city, but as soon as you get out into the country."

When breakfast was over, and Judy was washing up, Philip said to her, "Judy, why don't you stay here a week or two? That'll give you a chance to work out what to do next. It's no inconvenience to me, really." He hoped she would stay. He hadn't realised how comforting it was to have someone else in the house.

She smiled her winning smile, and stayed. They got on well. She listened carefully to his discussions of the books he was reading, and read the ones he recommended. She cooked meals and hoovered the floors and washed clothes and even wiped the windows so that all the smudges went away. She talked about the scenery of Western Australia, the desert, and the vineyards down on the Margaret River. She'd worked for a while in one. She smiled as she remembered. That must have been the good bit, thought Philip.

Three weeks later she crept into his bed one night, and things got a whole lot better. Philip had to admit to himself that his situation had turned out very well.

He asked Judy about herself. She was a little vague about her previous life, though she did tell him about her childhood in a coal-mining town in Fife. It had not been easy. Philip felt a little guilty about his own more comfortable upbringing.

The cottage had a small south-facing garden, and as the days became warmer, they sat out in it, reading or talking. At the end of the garden was a raised bed, surrounded by a stone wall about two feet high. There was a lot of cement between the stones, and it sloped down a bit at one end. "Darren built it himself," said Judy.

Philip felt a pang of jealousy. "Did he grow anything in it?"

he asked.

"No, he never got round to that. I think he found building it more interesting."

"Then we'll have to see what we can grow," said Philip. I'll achieve what Darren couldn't, he thought.

"The soil looks awfully poor," said Judy. "Lots of clay, by the look of it." She picked out a lump to show him, and tossed it back in. "I think you should just leave it, you could easily do yourself an injury trying to dig it over. Why don't we wait and see what wild flowers grow in it? Maybe they would attract butterflies."

One sunny day, when Judy had taken his car to go to the supermarket, he decided to have a go at digging over the raised bed. The only wild flowers he could see on it looked like weeds, and it needed tidying up. He got a trowel, and started in one corner. He found the soil wasn't as heavy as he'd expected. Darren must have spent some time preparing it. If he hadn't moved away, he might have got round to growing something.

He had got about three feet along, when a lump came up that didn't give when he poked it. It looked like a dried-up dog poo, but it didn't crumble. It might be something interesting, he thought, and ran it under the outside tap. As the clinging brown clay washed off, he saw it was a finger. A human finger. Not fossilised or mummified, not fresh either, but browned somewhat by the earth. Maybe a little finger, ragged at the base. It occurred to him that he may have chopped it off himself. Was there a hand, one finger short, in the earth there in front of him? A passing shiver raised the hairs at the back of his neck. How long since he'd felt that sensation?

But before he could explore any further, the back door opened, and Judy came out with mugs of tea on a tray. He hadn't heard the car come back.

She put the tray on the bench that faced the sun. He showed her what he'd found.

"Ugh!" she said. "It's revolting. A crow must have brought it here, dropped it on the bed. Maybe it had been to the tip – that's not that far away, or the cemetery. I think you should get rid of it. It's creepy."

"No. I don't think a crow brought it."

"A cat, then?"

"No. I think I chopped it off when I was digging. With the trowel. it's quite sharp, you see. The rest of the hand might be down there. Once I've had this tea, I'll have a look. Then I suppose we'll have to go to the police. They'll work out where it came from."

She said nothing, and they sat in silence, drinking the tea.

But mugs, even those inscribed 'A book is for ever,' are not bottomless. Sooner or later the tea runs out.

Philip stood up. "Well, back to work!" he said.

"Please, Philip." She put her hand on his arm. "Sit down, love."

He sat down again. "Whatever is it? If you bumped the car, don't worry, it won't be the first time it's had a bash." But he knew it wasn't the car. He could tell from her expression. He knew it was about the finger. A thought had crossed his mind, the sort of joke you make when you find something odd, but he'd pushed it away.

"It's Darren," she said. "He's in there. That's his finger."

"You mean, he's dead?" He heard himself. He sounded like a half-wit. "Maybe he had an accident." He tried hard to think of a way in which someone could have accidentally been buried in a raised bed. Perhaps Darren had dug a trench down the middle, then had a heart attack and fell into it twisting as he did so, so that the earth on either side fell in and covered him. No, it wasn't very convincing.

"I killed him, Philip," she said flatly. "I knew you'd find him sooner or later. As soon as the weather improved."

"You'd better tell me how it happened," he said.

"It was last June. We were in the garden. He was digging the soil in the raised bed over, just like you were. He thought of planting potatoes. I told him he was too late, he should have done it earlier. He got angry very easily, did Darren. Got into some fights that way. He told me to shut my mouth, threw a mug of tea at me, not the mug, just the hot tea. Then flung the mug onto the paving round the raised bed. It smashed. One I'd bought him for his birthday. Even had his name on it. 'Darren's Birthday Mug' it said." She stopped talking, stared at the ground.

"What happened next?"

"He just turned round and started digging again, with the trowel. There was a spade propped against the house wall. I picked it up as quietly as I could and hit him on the top of his head, as hard as I could. He just fell over onto the soil in the bed. Then I climbed into the bed, pushed his head down into the soil, and sat on it. He didn't move at all. I may have already killed him with the spade, I don't know. I couldn't move him, I mean, he was a big guy, and quite fat too. So I got the spade – I washed it first – and dug the soil bit by bit from under him and put it on top. It took hours, but eventually he had just disappeared, as if he'd never been there."

"So you decided not to tell the police?"

"I don't want to go to prison, Philip. I couldn't pretend it was an accident, could I? And besides,...well it doesn't matter. So no, I decided to cover it up. I knew it would come out sooner or later, but I wasn't thinking ahead."

Philip found that his initial horror was being overtaken by curiosity. "How did you manage to cover it up? Wouldn't people notice he'd disappeared?"

"Next morning I phoned his employers, said he was ill, he wouldn't be in for a few days. Then I booked a last-minute weekend in Spain."

"You went on holiday?"

"I just wanted to get away from the house. Well, not just that. While I was there I wrote a few letters, I mean I printed them from my laptop and signed them – I could do his signature quite well. So from a Spanish address, which I just made up – but the Spanish stamps and postmarks were real – he wrote, resigning his job, saying he'd decided to spend a few months in Spain, and telling them exactly what he thought of them. He'd told me that often enough himself. Then he wrote to the bank, telling them he couldn't keep up the payments on the house and they could sell it off if they wanted, and put any money owing to him into my account. Finally he wrote me a letter saying he was finished with me and telling me – in very unpleasant terms – to get out of his house. I knew his log-in details so he emailed a few friends saying he'd got a job in Spain and wouldn't be around for a few months. Luckily his parents don't speak to him – they cut him off after he got sent to prison the first time, and the same goes for his sister, so they wouldn't come looking for him. Then, once I'd got back, I emailed my own friends to say he'd thrown me out and then gone to Spain. I moved in with one of them for a couple of weeks to sort things out and sell the car. Then I went to Australia."

"Which didn't work out?"

"I got work in the vineyard for a few months, and that was OK, but I didn't have the right kind of visa, so I couldn't stay. To be honest, I was getting a bit fed up anyway. They paid me a pittance, and I found the place just too dry. I missed the rain, how daft is that?" She smiled her winning smile, but Philip didn't notice.

"Why come back here?" he asked. "I mean, why didn't you just move somewhere completely different? Why come to me?"

"I realised that Darren's body would be found as soon as somebody started fiddling with the raised bed. So I decided to find out who was living here, see if they were likely to do that."

"So bursting into my life in the middle of the night, that was all deliberate?"

"Yes, I'm sorry. I'd found out you were here on your own and wanted to check you out, see what kind of person you were. I thought you were someone who wouldn't bother too much about his garden."

"You were right. I wouldn't have done anything with that raised bed if you hadn't been here."

"What happened after that wasn't planned. I found you were more than that. You were a home for me. Not the house. You, Philip. You still are, and I'm sorry to have involved you in all this. I wish things had been different."

"We all do that at times, but it doesn't achieve anything, does it? Things are as they are and we make the best of them." Philip paused. He knew the sensible thing was to call the police and tell them everything. That would be fine for him, of course, it was Judy who'd be locked up for years. He didn't have to think too long to realise that he couldn't live with that. Her life was in his hands. He looked at her, and he knew that she knew it too. Now she wasn't smiling, and all at once she dropped the mug so that it, like Darren's, smashed on the paving.

He opened his mouth, and heard himself speak. "I like having you in my home, Judy, in my life. I don't think I could go back to what it was like before. I'd like you to stay here."

"I'd like that too, Philip. So much so. But what about…?" She gestured at the bed.

"Yes," said Philip, "the soil there needs topping up quite a bit, we'll need to buy some bags of compost. Then I think I'll just plant radishes. I don't need to dig too deep for them. Oh, and maybe we should go somewhere hot for a few days, and Darren could write some more letters."

A Walk by the River

Hugh Westertoun liked walking by the river. As a sixth-year student, he was free to leave the Community High School campus whenever he had free time. And since he was only taking Maths and Physics at Advanced Higher level, plus German at Standard Grade, he had plenty free time. Not that he spent all of it walking by the river; he was seen in the school library often enough by his teachers to satisfy them of his dedication to learning. And as Sixth-years didn't have to wear uniform, he could be anywhere in the town without standing out.

But the riverbank was his favourite place. He wasn't particularly sociable. The Fourth Year girls' discussion group, whose main topic was the opposite sex, judged him uninteresting, though 'weirdo' and 'geek' were heard, with little evidence offered, and a minority opinion held that he wasn't even interested in girls. He preferred being by the riverbank on his own, preferably in the afternoon, when the river seemed to have settled into its mode of being for the day.

There was a well-made path by the riverside. It was known as Queen Margaret's Walk, after a legend which recalled that the sainted wife of Malcolm III, whilst sojourning here, no doubt on the lookout for good causes, had, whilst walking by the riverside, encountered a river-spirit. The spirit emerged from the river in the shape of a dreadful beast, half bear and half dragon, and threatened to tear the saintly monarch in pieces and feast upon them. The lady, with commendable humility, invited the creature to go ahead, saving only that it leave her head behind, so that she would be recognised, and her husband could offer her remains a proper Christian burial. The creature, advancing upon her with enormous claws outstretched, suddenly found himself – these aggressive and uninhibited monstrosities do tend to be male – stuck to the ground. And more than that, he felt himself being sucked downwards into the earth, for the riverbank itself could not allow an innocent woman, and especially one whose holiness radiated around her, to be killed and eaten by such a dreadful being. Writhing and squirming, the creature sank deeper into the mud and stones of the riverside path, until only its head was visible. Now it pleaded with the queen for mercy, promising never to eat humans again and, indeed, even to become a vegetarian if that would do the trick. The saint only smiled beatifically, observing quietly, "All nature moves at His command," as the head slowly sank out of sight and the pathway closed over it, burying the creature alive for all eternity, to suffocate in earthen darkness until the End of Days.

The Walk followed the river for perhaps three quarters of a mile, then turned inland to return to the town by a rather featureless country road. Hugh found the road tedious and preferred to walk up the river to the point where the path turned inland and then return following the river again. He found that walking against the river's flow, and then back alongside it gave him an enhanced awareness, as if seen from two different viewpoints, of the river's nature. Its water was always brown, either a deep and clear brown, coloured by the peaty soil through which moisture dripped and trickled to find its way into the burns which fed its headwaters, or a lighter, more opaque and perhaps more sinister brown, made by the mud and earth clawed into itself by the river as it moved across the wide strath on its way to the firth and the open sea. Hugh could thus term each day a day of peat or a day of mud.

This day was a day of mud. There had been rain on the previous days, and the sudden increase in volume had forced the moving water against the banks, sucking earth, stones, branches, and all manner of buried objects into its current, to be held like treasures or stolen loot and borne downstream until reluctantly relinquished. The water level was high, and it seemed to Hugh as if all sorts of creatures slunk and oozed beneath the river's bloated countenance, visible only as pulsations or swirlings of the water. As he began his return journey, this sense of ugly heavings and slumpings just below the water's sallow and unhealthy skin increased, until, after about a hundred yards, he came to a stop, and could only stare at the unending mass of water moving by him.

It was a place where some large boulders had been pulled from the bank almost into midstream, and the water moved sleekly over them, a continuous skein of moving water smoothing and masking the contours of the stones. He could even imagine that these were not stones, but living creatures, hump-backed and savage aquatic life-forms from another age, lying in wait for the innocent passer-by, be it fish or fowl or four-legged mammal. He stood so long, indeed, that he imagined the rounded carapaces with their bulging eyes gradually turning their blank unwavering gaze on him, their only witness.

His reverie was disturbed by some small animal in the corner of his vision. It scuttled in front of him, oblivious to his presence, revealing itself to be a small black fluffy dog, of the kind that will bark without any prompting, and ran on towards the river, bounded onto the narrow beach of pebbles eroded from the bank, and began to lap at the water.

Immediately a long tooth-filled jaw yawned up from the water in front of it, and slammed shut, capturing the dog within. Hugh was frozen to the spot. A crocodile! And a big one too. It paused, its unblinking eyes encompassing him, sizing him up. Then deciding that a dog in the hand is worth hanging on to, it turned away, now revealing its short but powerful legs and hand-like feet, and its large body, gnarled and slimy, and slithered back into the muddy water. In a few seconds it was gone.

As he stood, transfixed by what he had seen, a couple came round the bend in the path towards him. The man, perhaps around forty – Hugh wasn't good on ages – had a shaven head, his arms covered in tattoos, and glasses with thick lenses, and wore a T-shirt with a skull on it and blue jeans. The woman with him seemed much younger, much closer to his own age. She was thin, with long dark straggling hair, a pale face with a sad expression, and a slight limp. She wore blue jeans too, and a light blue top, carried a black shoulder bag, and was clutching a dog lead in her right hand.

The man strode up to Hugh. "Hey, pal, seen a wee black dug around here? The stupid cow here let it off the lead." He nodded dismissively towards the woman, who looked at the ground.

Hugh was still in a bit of daze. "It was a crocodile. It came out of the river and grabbed it. Then swam away."

"A crocodile?" said the man. "Yer jokin, pal?"

"No. That's what it was. A crocodile."

"So you're sayin a crocodile came out the water, ate her dug, and ran away?"

"Yes," said Hugh. "That's what happened. I'm sorry. About the dog, I mean. There was nothing I could..."

The blow caught him completely unawares. The man had punched him hard in the stomach. He doubled up, fell onto the muddy path, groaning.

"Don't you fuckin joke with me, ya bastard," shouted the man. "Now, tell me where the bloody dug is or I'll kick yer fuckin head in."

Hugh thought fast. "Alright! The dog jumped into the river and swam across. It's probably in the grass at the other side."

"That's better." The man aimed a kick at Hugh's chest, but he had squirmed round and the foot hit his thigh instead.

"Leave him alone, please, Ray!" called the woman, "If Toby's over there we need to get him back."

"Aye, all right," grumbled the man, "ah'll get the wee moron."

He turned away from Hugh, as if he no longer existed, and went down to the narrow beach of pebbles. He sat down on the bank, took his shoes and socks off, and threw them onto the bank. Then he stepped into the water and began, stepping very tentatively, to wade across.

Hugh had managed to sit upright. He was thinking he should get away before the man found the dog wasn't there and came back for him again. He was beginning to lever himself onto his feet when he heard a shout, and the woman screamed. She was staring at the river. Hugh looked too. The man was lying on his back on the stones that stood above the water. But his legs were clamped in the crocodile's jaws. The creature shook its great head, pulling the man clear of the rocks, then it crawled into the water, dragging him after it. He gave one more scream before disappearing as the beast rolled over in the water, pulling him under. Then it swam away, sinking beneath the surface, so that only its wake was visible, moving rapidly down the river and out of sight round the bend.

Hugh pulled himself to his feet and staggered over towards the woman. She stood as if she were a statue, staring at the water. Then she seemed to notice the lead in her hand. "Toby!" she wailed. "My poor Toby. Poor Toby. Where will I find him now?"

Hugh didn't know how to deal with the situation. "Are you all right?" he said to the young woman, knowing perfectly well that she wasn't. He came up to her, and she put her arms around him and held tight. He could feel her sobs, shuddering from head to foot, shaking the painfully thin body he was holding. Instinctively he held her tighter. He thought the screams would have attracted other strollers along the riverbank, but no-one appeared. He was aware that Tuesday afternoon was a slack time for walkers. Were they all at Aldi or the Co-op?

His mind swung back to the crocodile. It was a crocodile, he had no doubt about that. How it had got there, how long it had been there, he had no idea. He'd heard of cases where people had got baby crocs from pet-shops, then when they started to get bigger, tried to dispose of them. Certainly, throwing an unwanted aquatic pet into the nearest river was better than flushing it down the toilet. He guessed it must have been there for years to get that big. Or did they grow quickly? Or had it escaped from a zoo or a wildlife park, and made its way across country to find the nearest water?

He felt the woman shift, and she pulled away from him slightly. "I want to go home now," she said quietly.

"Shall I come with you?" Hugh said. "To make sure you get there all right?"

"Yes, if you want," she answered. "Please, keep holding me."

He moved one arm away and slid the other round her shoulders, so they could walk along together. He sensed she was still in some sort of shock. She moved as if sleepwalking, not looking to left or right, and not really seeing what was ahead, so that he sometimes had to guide her around obstacles, an interpretation board, a bollard, a jogger. Cradled in his arm, she seemed to him now even younger than she had at first, almost like a child perplexed by events beyond her understanding.

When they got back to the beginning of Queen Margaret's Walk, at the edge of the town, she seemed to sense where she was, and moved out of his arm. "It's this way," she whispered, and walked in the same sleepy sort of way past the entrance to the park and up the hill towards the older part of the town. Then she turned left into a street of stone-fronted three-storey tenements opening directly onto the pavement. Not the fine red sandstone tenements you'd see in Glasgow's West End; these were of a pale grey stone, eroded in some parts, and flaking in others. The windows looked neglected, and there were plants growing in the gutter along the edge of the roof.

"It's number twenty-three," she said, "just along here. I'm on the top floor."

The close was gloomy and smelt of food that had gone bad. The stone stairs were old and worn and narrow. On the top floor, there were two doors. She led him to the one on the right. 'Flat 2' was written in biro on a card stuck to the door with a drawing pin. "Here we are," she said, "I expect Toby will be waiting for me." She fumbled in her bag for the key.

The flat was small and worn-out and cold, and Toby wasn't there. The woman slumped into an ancient armchair in the living-room-cum-kitchen and stared at the dull grey bars of the electric fire. Hugh wondered what to do next. Warmth. He switched on the fire. Hot coffee, isn't that what people who've had a shock get? Or alcohol. He filled the kettle and switched it on. Then looked in the cupboards for coffee or alcohol. There was a jar of cheap instant coffee from the pound shop they'd passed on the way up. And a half-empty bottle of vodka. There was milk in the fridge, so he made two mugs of coffee, added a generous dash of vodka to one of them, then passed it to her.

She took it without looking at him. He was afraid she'd drop it, but finally she raised it to her lips and took a sip. That seemed to stimulate her a little. "Toby's gone, isn't he?" she muttered.

"Yes, I'm afraid so," said Hugh.

She took another sip. "And Ray, he's gone too?"

"Yes, he's gone too."

"I never liked Ray. He could be nice when he wanted to be, but most of the time he didn't want to be. He hit me, you know, all over, and not just when he drank, it could be any time. Half the time I never knew why, he had some grudge that never came to the surface, but it burned inside him. No wonder his wife threw him out." She took a longer drink of the coffee. "This is good. Thank you." Now she looked at Hugh. "I'm sorry, I don't know who you are."

"My name's Hugh Westertoun. We live further up the hill, above Main Street. I'm, er, at the High School. I was just walking by the river when I saw what happened."

"I'm Suzanne. Thank you for helping me. I don't know what I'd have done if you'd not been there. I'm sorry about Ray hitting you. He shouldn't have done that."

"Look, Suzanne. We'll have to report this. I mean, what with Ray being, em, gone, and that thing in the river. To the police, I suppose."

"No! Not the police. I've had enough trouble with them already. I called them once when Ray had…done something I didn't want. And they weren't interested. Then Ray said I was making it up and they took his side. They all had a big laugh about it, that's what Ray said afterwards."

"But if Ray's disappeared, it has to be reported."

"No, it doesn't. No one will miss him. He didn't have a job. He wasn't recorded at this address. I'm the only occupant, to get the single person's council tax rate. So he's not on the electoral roll, and he doesn't have a bank account, or anything that links him to here."

"Didn't he have friends who'd miss him?"

"Friends weren't Ray's style. He managed to fall out with everybody he knew. I guess there will be people he drank with, but I doubt he'll have told them where he lived. He'd be afraid of someone grassing to the council. Honest, Hugh, it'll be like he never existed. I can get rid of all his stuff tomorrow."

"But what about the crocodile? Surely we should warn them about it?"

She drained the last of the coffee. "Do you really think they'd believe us? 'Please, sergeant, there's a crocodile in the river and it ate my partner.' What do you think would happen next? I'll tell you. I'd certainly be arrested for murder and you'd be arrested as an accessory. The fact there's no body won't stop us being sent to jail. And if the croc leaves a few bits somewhere, that'll only prove that we cut up his body and threw the pieces in the river. Any teeth marks would be attributed to a pike or something like that. Then you'd be charged with murder too. Don't you see that?"

Hugh had to admit that he did see it. So there was nothing to be done. "What'll you do, Suzanne? Do you have enough money?"

She laughed. "You don't imagine Ray produced any cash. He was a sponger, a parasite. I wish I'd never met him. At least now I can forget him. I'm okay for money, thanks, Hugh. I work at the pound shop. The pay's not good, but it'll keep me alive. And don't worry yourself, I've no intention of topping myself out of grief for Ray. Or for Toby, for that matter. My life doesn't belong to either of them. What about another coffee?"

Hugh made her another coffee, but turned down one for himself. He realised it was now nearly five o'clock, and he'd need to get home soon. All the more so, as, if the matter were not going to be reported, this must look like a perfectly ordinary day. He wrote his address and mobile number on a page torn from his diary – the first time he'd ever torn a page out – and gave it to her. "Just in case you need anything."

As he stood in the narrow hallway, waiting for Suzanne to open the door, she put her arms around him, and kissed him, first on the cheek and then gently on the lips. She must have stood on tiptoes to do that he thought, as he breathed the distant smell of something exotic that emanated from her skin and her hair. "Thank you, Hugh," she said, "I needed you today. You're a good man, don't ever forget that."

He hesitated in the open doorway. "Er, maybe I could pop in next Tuesday afternoon, just see how things are?"

"Yes, that would be nice," she said.

He walked home, feeling as if he had visited another universe, and hadn't quite come back yet. It started raining, and he was well-soaked by the time he got home. The other universe had been washed off him by then. But not out of his mind.

He looked in the papers as the days passed, but there was no mention of Ray's disappearance, or any sightings of a crocodile.

The following Tuesday he went round to Suzanne's flat. No-one answered his knocking at the door. But the door opposite opened, and an old woman appeared. "What is it you want?" she asked.

"I was hoping Suzanne was in, and..."

"What's your name, son?"

"Er, Hugh."

"Suzanne's away, son. She moved out two days ago, on Sunday. She didna have much to take with her, just the one case. Told me she was going up north, Inverness way. Get a new life. That Ray was no use for her. She told me he'd buggered off down south somewhere. Good riddance, eh? But just you wait there a wee minute."

She shuffled back into her hallway and reappeared a minute later, with an A4-sized envelope. "She gave me this to pass on to you. She said you'd be here this afternoon."

On a bench in the park Hugh opened the envelope. In it was a sketch, in pencil, of himself. It was a good one, he thought, somehow she'd got under his skin. It was signed in the corner, Suzanne xx. There was a thank-you card too, with a note written inside: 'Dear Hugh, I'm sorry you won't find me here. I decided to move away, start over again. Thank you for everything. I won't forget you. Suzanne xx'

Only the Fourth Year girls' discussion group noticed the change in Hugh. His epithets now became 'mysterious' and 'enigmatic' and a minority opinion claimed she was in love with him.

Two weeks later, Hugh noticed a report in the paper. A fisherman had disappeared, near a village some twenty-odd miles further down the river. No trace of him had been found, and the police appealed for help. It was thought he was standing, in his waders, in the centre of the river, and might have lost his footing and been swept away by the unusually high water.

From the Casebook of Sally McInnes

Trouble with Chickens

I wakened up when the phone rang early. I knew it was early because it woke me up, and I usually wake about half seven. I was also in the middle of dreaming and I'm usually finished that when I wake up. My dream was about zombies. I can't remember what they were doing, but it wasn't polite.

Neither was my caller. "Miss McIsaac, be so good as to get your ass down here, we've got a dead man." Inspector Gillen. He always had to drag other peace-loving citizens into his investigations. OK, I work for him, but did he really need me at six o'clock in the morning?

"No problemo, chief. Where's here?" No good grumbling, you've got to seem willing. He's not going to let me back to bed whatever I do. And why he insists on calling me 'Miss' rather than 'Sergeant'…

"Meikle Powhead. It's a cottage on the B9037, near Torryburn, about five miles west of Rosyth. You can't miss it, there'll be flashing lights outside."

That was my breakfast off the menu, so I got myself ready, grabbed a couple of muesli bars and headed out.

There's not a lot of traffic out there at six, the Edinburgh rush is just beginning to get under way, so it didn't take me long to get there. It was June, so it was daylight by then. The flashing lights were still useful though.

The place was on a kind of lay-by, which I guessed was where the road went before it was straightened up in the sixties or seventies. Two police cars and a white forensics van were already there, as well as Gillen's gleaming silver BMW. The house looked like the usual sort of farm cottage, door at the centre, one window at each side, gable at each end of the building. To the right was a garage of rusty corrugated iron. A car was parked in front of it, an old Toyota. The front garden, if there ever was one, had reverted to nature, but my colleagues had helped the cause of civilisation by trampling much of it down.

Forensics had even put up a tent, so I popped in there to get some plastic overshoes and nitrile gloves. Jenny O'Riordan was sat behind a fold-up table, typing stuff into a laptop. There was a pile of evidence bags on the table. "Sally, it's yourself!" she said. "You'll love this one, sure you will." She dropped the evidence bag she'd been registering into a cardboard box and selected another from the pile.

"Oh, yeah, why's that, Jenny?"

"I wouldn't want to spoil the moment, Sally. Just get yourself in there and take a peep."

"Where's the stiff?"

"Front room, on the left."

I headed for the front door. Two uniforms who'd been lounged by the front door chatting straightened up. "Morning, er, Sarge," one of them muttered.

There was a board hung on the door, with "FRESH EGGS – RING BELL" painted on it. As soon as I touched the handle it opened and I was face-to-face with Gillen. He looked into my eyes, I looked into his brain. His moustache twitched. "About time," he grunted. "Did you walk here?"

"Very amusing, chief. If only I had a BMW I'd be here in no time. What have we got?"

"I told you already. Dead male."

"Murder?"

I went into the tiny hallway – walls painted brown didn't help the sense of space – then took the door on the left. The room had once been a living-room or parlour. There was a fireplace at the gable end and a bed recess in the rear wall. In the recess stood two full-height fridges, side by side. The only other furniture in the room was a long wooden table, with a single upright wooden chair behind it.

An old man was sitting on the chair, but the top half of his body was slumped forward onto the table. His head was face down in a steep-sided frying pan about three inches deep. Maybe it was called something else – omelette pan, sauté pan, who knows. The pan wasn't empty, and the man's face was embedded in thick yellow liquid, on the surface of which a skin had formed. The bit of his head you could see was bald with sparse white hair sticking out around the edge.

"It's egg." Gillen had come in behind me. "Looks like he was making a big omelette, had beaten up the eggs, had a heart attack, dropped his head into the egg." Gillen liked cases to be closed nice and simply. Good for the statistics. He lived by the clear-up rate. He wanted to make DCI soon. Maybe he was finding it hard to keep up the payments on his car.

"What does the doc think?"

"The doc thinks he's dead. Might be heart attack, might have drowned."

"Drowned in raw egg. That's one you don't get too often. Have you considered suicide?"

"We can't rule that out either, of course."

The fact that Gillen was prepared to believe the man had beaten up two dozen or so eggs, then rested his face in them till he was dead, tells you plenty about Gillen, but doesn't advance the investigation.

"Perhaps it was a bizarre beauty therapy that went wrong."

Gillen grabbed at that one too. "Yes. That's certainly another possibility. That would account for him bringing the pan through here from the kitchen, and for the number of eggs used. I did think two dozen was a lot for omelette, or even scrambled egg. Unless he cut it into batches, put them in the freezer."

"Eggs don't freeze well," I said. "I tried it." I walked round the table.

"Watch the eggshells!" warned Gillen. I saw what he meant. They were littered on the worn red carpet, around the table.

"Even the most careless among us don't throw our eggshells on the floor," I observed.

"Unless it was suicide." He didn't give up easily.

I opened the fridge on the right. It was stacked with cardboard trays of eggs. I picked an egg out. It had "MP" written on the base with a thick red felt pen. Meikle Powhead. "He must have plenty chickens," I said. "By the way, who is he?"

"George Cowell, widowed, lives alone here, owns the house. His daughter – she lives in Peterhead – phoned him last night, got no answer. Thought he might have gone to bed early, worried herself into a state during the night, phoned us about five o'clock. Nothing much doing for the night shift, so somebody popped round, took a look in the front window, saw him right away. Mind you, he was 79, old enough to drop dead at any moment."

"So why were his hands held down?" I had lifted one of the claw-like hands from the table, and looked at the fingernails. "His nails have scored the polish here – he was trying to lift his hands."

Gillen looked shifty. "I'd have seen that on the forensic report. Peters is writing it up in the kitchen at the moment." Gillen didn't believe in doing something for himself if someone else would do it. That included examining a crime scene. He called it delegation.

"And look at this," I went on, "a couple of faint bruises either side of his head. Two guys did this. One held his hands down on the table, while the other held his head and pushed it into the pan, held him down till he drowned."

"Those forensics people are so slow," he said. "I should have known this by the time you got here. We pay them too much, they get lazy. We'll need to get these uniforms into action, too."

I'd heard this often enough. I went through to the kitchen. The table for one and the cosy armchair told me this was where George Cowell spent most of his time. Greg Peters was sat at the table, pecking at a laptop.

"Any prints?" I said.

"Not a sausage. But we got a hair in the egg. Short, blond. And a tyre track outside. Jenny'll show you. I need to get this report done for Gillen."

I went out and walked round the cottage. A uniformed PC was standing by the back door, peering at his phone. "Where are the chickens?" I asked him.

"I dunno, Sarge. Not seen any."

"See if you can find a coop, they should be active by now, probably need fed. I'll check the garage."

The rickety door at the side of the garage had been recently forced. Inside, the place was chaotic. All sorts of things everywhere. Bits of furniture, car parts, garden tools, flower pots, an old bicycle, a black bag full of old newspapers. A smell of decay and disuse, but no chicken food. Or chickens.

There was another smell, too, a bit like turpentine. I noticed something gleam on the floor, something without a layer of dust. A can lying on its side in the puddle which was giving off the smell. I knelt down to look at it – some sort of solvent, I didn't recognise the name. Maybe he'd been doing some painting.

I met the uniform as I came out. "No sign of any chicken-house, Sarge. Or any chickens either. Maybe whoever killed him pinched them. Chicken rustlers. Fife's answer to big-time crime." He grinned inanely.

"What's your name, Constable?" I asked him.

"Rankin, Sarge."

"You'll go far, Constable, report it to Inspector Gillen."

I had another look round. PC Rankin was right. No chickens. I had an idea, and went back into the house. I could hear Gillen in the kitchen: "Killed for his chickens?" he was saying. "Can you believe it?"

An ambulance must have arrived. The door to the other room was open and a couple of paramedics were getting Cowell's body off his chair. His face was visible now, the wet egg hanging to it like a damp shroud. I went round to the fridges and opened the left-hand one. It contained twelve-packs of eggs, with a well-known supermarket brand-name. I opened one up and looked at the eggs. Each one had a number stamped on the base. Some sort of quality-control mark.

I went out the front door and into the forensics tent. I asked Jenny about the tyre track. "Yes, pretty recent, and quite distinct, just off the lay-by. We've got a 3-D scan. Maybe a Range Rover."

I asked Jenny to check the solvent can for prints, and went back into the house.

"D'you hear that?" said Gillen, from the kitchen doorway. "Killed for a few chickens. Some neds from the Edinburgh slums, no doubt. Or immigrants. Eastern Europeans. Moroccans. They all eat chicken, don't they?"

"The chickens were never here," I said.

"What do you mean?"

"There weren't any chickens. He bought the eggs in a supermarket, used some solvent to take off the stamp, put the initials of this place – MP – over the top in case there was any mark left, and pretended the eggs were from his own chickens. Sold them at twice the price to unsuspecting passers-by."

"So why kill him, if it weren't for the chickens?"

"They didn't take the eggs either," put in Peters.

"Maybe someone topped him for faking farm eggs," suggested Rankin.

"Don't be ridiculous!" snapped Gillen. "Look to those closest," he pronounced, "Maybe it was a family feud."

"He has a married son," said Peters. "He lives…"

"Bring him in!" interrupted Gillen. "We've been barking up the wrong tree here."

"I was going to say," said Peters quietly, "that he lives in New Zealand."

"Ah. OK. McIsaac, any ideas." That was Gillen's problem; he was very short on ideas. When he noticed the deficit, that was when he usually turned to me.

"I don't suppose you read *Scotlandshire* magazine, sir?" I said. "The one that usually has dead animals on the front, or men in wellies?"

Gillen bridled. "As a matter of fact, I do, and I don't like your implication about the covers. That's game, not dead animals. In any case, what's that got to do with anything?"

"You may remember an article that was in it about three months ago. I don't buy it myself, but I like to check through the glossy magazines each month, in the library, just in case there's anything of local interest that's worth remembering. As background."

"What article are you talking about, Sergeant? They certainly don't have features in *Scotlandshire* about chickens. There was one on poaching – could Cowell have been taking deer?"

"No. There was a feature about someone who lives not far from here – Dmitry Rossinov. Have you come across him?"

"Yes, of course. Pillar of the community. Successful businessman in Russia, exiled by Putin when he fell out with him. I've met him a couple of times at various events. Nice man. Very generous to good causes. Actually, I do remember that piece about him – an interview, wasn't it? He was very complimentary about the fishing in Scotland, I think."

"Yes, that's right, chief. I photocopied the article. I don't have the copy with me, but I can remember the broad outlines. His estate near here is quite large. He likes to keep fit, swims, rides, lifts weights, shoots. He talks about his diet, how he only eats things freshly produced locally, and guaranteed organic."

"What's that got to do with anything?"

"I'm just saying we should maybe check him out. You see, chief, I've read other stuff about Rossinov that's not so complimentary. He owned a soft drinks factory somewhere to the south east of Moscow. Two years ago one of the ingredients in their cola drink killed twenty-two people and left another two hundred on medication for the rest of their lives. Apparently people at the plant had known about it, but Rossinov's enforcers kept them quiet. After the poisonings, the cynical use of toxic ingredients was so obvious the authorities had to act. But of course they warned him in advance, so he and his money could get out of the country in time."

"I've not seen any of this in the newspapers."

"No, chief, you wouldn't. But it's all there online. Al Jezeera, France 24, even Russia Today reported it."

"But how would he know about the eggs being faked?"

"Maybe one of his people saw Cowell buying the eggs. He wouldn't do it locally, probably across the bridge at one of the Edinburgh shopping centres. Or perhaps he just wondered why there were no chickens around. Would have made more sense for Cowell to keep a few, just for appearances."

"You're surely not suggesting he killed this man Cowell just for faking fresh eggs."

"Rossinov is a man who doesn't like being embarrassed or swindled. He takes revenge. And it's often very nasty."

"I suppose we'd better go and see him, then," said Gillen, looking worried.

The entrance to Rossinov's estate was about six miles further west. When we arrived in Gillen's car, the heavy iron gates were firmly closed. All we could see beyond was a narrow drive turning sharply into thick woodland. But in a moment they began to swing open. "Ah, they've seen us," muttered Gillen. But as he swung his car into the open gateway another vehicle emerged from the woods at some speed and skidded to a halt right in front of us. The driver gesticulated at us, waving us back towards the road.

"He's in a hurry," I said.

"We better see what he's up to," said Gillen.

As we got out, the driver's door of the Range Rover opened, and a big man with a pasty face, short blond hair, and a hostile expression, emerged. "Private estate!" he shouted. "Get out! Or I throw you out." He spoke with a heavy East European accent.

Gillen is conscious of his status, doesn't like dealing with servants. He leaves that to me.

"Police," I said, holding up my ID card. "May I see you driving licence, sir, it won't take a moment."

The thug was puzzled. "Private estate!" he shouted again, and started forward, looking more unpleasant.

The rear door of the Range Rover opened and a man in an expensive suit got out. He was tall and well-built, with immaculately-cut dark hair and a moustache that a 1930s matinee idol would have been proud of. In the sunlight his shoes gleamed, his white shirt sparkled, his silk tie glowed warmly. He ignored me and smiled at Gillen. "I'm so sorry," he said – his English was good – "but my driver does not understand English, or should I say, Scottish, so well." He spoke a few words, in Russian I assumed, to his henchman. I only caught the first: 'Bariss'. I think that's Boris to us. The man nodded and returned to station himself by the car door.

Gillen introduced himself and showed his ID. "You are perhaps Mr Rossinov?"

"Yes, that's correct. I think I've met you before, Inspector. At the Golf Club, perhaps? Such a relaxing game, don't you think? Now, I'm afraid I'm in a hurry – I need to get to the airport, I have a meeting this morning in Amsterdam. So if you go on up to the house my head of security will be happy to deal with whatever you want. I'll give him a ring now, then we can be on our way."

As I said, Gillen is conscious of his status. He doesn't take easily to a brush-off. "I'm afraid it's yourself we wish to talk to, Mr Rossinov."

"Surely, Inspector, this can wait. As I said, I have a plane to catch. If you go to the house…"

"I'm sorry, sir, but we need to talk now," insisted Gillen. "We are investigating the murder of George Cowell, who is a neighbour of yours."

"I keep myself to myself," said Rossinov. "I have been in my house for the past two days. My staff will confirm this. Is there anything else?"

"Thank you," said Gillen. "We will of course need to take statements from all of you. And, of course, DNA samples. Simply to exclude you from our inquiries. We're asking the same from all Mr Cowell's neighbours."

Rossinov's smile disappeared. "I'm in a hurry," he said icily, "and I will not be held up by little bureaucrats. I told you to speak to my head of security. Now, please get out of my way. Or would you prefer me to call your superiors?" He nodded to Boris to get into the car and did so himself.

While this was going on I had discreetly radioed for one of our cars at Cowell's cottage to come over.

Rossinov's car reversed suddenly and attempted to drive past Gillen's, forcing him to jump out of the way, and smashing the rear light of the BMW as it squeezed past at speed. I thought they were about to get away, but just at that moment the heavy gates began to swing shut, and the Range Rover crashed into them. I realised they must be on a timer.

"The bastard!" gasped Gillen, picking himself up. "He's damaged my bloody car. My car!" He ran over to the rear door of the Range Rover and flung it open. But before he could do anything else a foot, in a polished leather shoe, shot out and caught him square in the stomach. He doubled up and disappeared out of sight. The Range Rover reversed again, and hit a tree. Rossinov and Boris both jumped out. Rossinov was on his phone and Boris made for me. He was big and fat and carrying a wheel wrench.

I retreated and looked for something to defend myself. I picked up a branch that had come off a tree by the gate. "Police!" I called but he kept on coming. As he came up to me, he raised the bar behind him. I'd played a lot of hockey in my youth, and you don't do that without learning how to take the feet from under an opponent. I cracked him on the ankles, and the momentum of his weapon helped to take him down on his back, where he lay groaning. A whack on the shins with my branch reminded him not to get up.

Rossinov's message to the house must have got through, as the gates swung open again. But at this moment the backup I'd called swung into the gateway, and four uniforms sprang out, ready for some aggro. I pointed to the recumbent Boris, and two of them were onto him in a flash, whipped him onto his front and slipped the cuffs on.

Meanwhile Rossinov, seeing what had happened, turned to make off up to his house. I swung the branch and knocked him off his feet too. "Cuff him as well!" I shouted to the uniforms. "Then take them both down to the station and book them for assault."

Gillen was trying to get back on his feet. "He ruined my bloody suit," he gasped, "as well as my car."

The tyre marks at the cottage matched Rossinov's Range Rover. A partial print Jenny found on the solvent can matched Boris, and the DNA match on the hair saw to his conviction for Cowell's murder. Unfortunately there wasn't enough of a case to prosecute Rossinov himself for the killing. He readily confessed to assaulting a police officer, although a tame doctor and psychologist argued he was suffering from a momentary "emotional perspective dysfunction." He was given a suspended sentence and fined a thousand pounds; he paid the fine immediately in cash, and left the courtroom smiling. However, the publicity had panicked his friends in the establishment: two months later his residence permit was rescinded, and he was put on a plane back to Russia as an 'undesirable alien.' On arrival he was arrested on corruption charges; his case didn't come to court and he was never seen again. Meanwhile, Inspector Gillen was acclaimed a hero and got his promotion.

And the moral of the tale: don't buy the eggs till you've seen the chickens.

Death by Chocolate

I'm often off on a Wednesday. Maybe there's less crime on Wednesdays. Especially in April, in Dunfermline. Or maybe Chief Inspector Gillen doesn't want to be dragged off the golf course or out of the Masonic Lodge by his enthusiastic subordinate. "You'll never get into the Masons," he told me once. "Well, obviously, you're a woman. But what I meant was, apart from that." When I asked exactly what he meant, he thought hard, then decided he had to go to a meeting.

That's why I was in when my neighbour Jackie MacMahon called. She was looking around furtively when I answered the door, and rushed in immediately. Didn't she want to be seen on my doorstep? Her hair was a bit windblown – I could see the grey at the roots. That could have been the walk to the door, or she could have been standing there a while debating whether to ring the bell.

I ushered her to a chair at the kitchen table. While I made the coffee she fidgeted, and stared out of the window.

"Are you looking for someone?" I asked, as I brought the coffee in.

"No, no, Sally, it's just that this is a bit, er, confidential. I wasn't sure whether I should tell you. But I mean, well, you being a policewoman..."

"Police officer," I corrected.

"Yes, yes, of course, well, you see, I think she's trying to kill him."

"OK Jackie, I think you'd better start at the beginning."

She took a minute or two to compose herself. "Yes, of course. It's my brother-in-law, I mean my husband's older brother, Walter, Walter MacMahon. He's two years older than David, so he'll be 55 now. Well, four years ago he got married. It was a real surprise, we all thought he was a confirmed bachelor."

"He hadn't been married before?"

"No. It's not that he's not interested in women. But he's quite shy, and a bit of a workaholic. He runs a financial consultancy, advising people how to avoid paying tax, you know, setting up dummy companies in the Cayman Islands, Swiss bank accounts, that sort of thing."

"Sounds like a lucrative business."
"Oh yes. David's quite jealous. Doesn't see why he should be slaving away in the classroom…"
"I thought he was a Depute Head."
"Yes, but it's hard work anyway."
"So Walter got married?"
"Yes. It was quite a whirlwind romance. He met her at a do one of his clients had organised. Two months later they were married. Here's a picture of them at the wedding." She pulled her iPhone from her handbag and with a few practised thumbstrokes found what she was looking for, laid the phone on the table. "See, there. That's Walter and Rebecca. She's quite a lot younger than him. We couldn't see what she saw in him. Except, of course, his money."
The happy couple stood in the centre of a group of overdressed grinning relatives, Jackie and David among them. Walter was a bookish-looking individual, quite tall and running a little to fat – there was a double chin beginning to emerge – but nothing too gross. He was bald and had a bushy moustache. And he wore thick glasses, which gave him an air of not quite knowing where he was. Indeed, in the picture he seemed to be grinning at somewhere to the left of the photographer. By contrast, his wife was slim and petite, with long blonde hair and a turned up nose. Her smile at the camera was perfect.
"Now look at this one," said Jackie. "It was taken at a recent family gathering, for our daughter's twenty-first." She slid the next picture over.
I caught my breath. Had I not been on my best behaviour, I would have loosed a few expletives. Instead, I managed a thoughtful, "Hmm, there's quite a difference." This time the couple were sat at a table with an impressive and colourful display of food ranged before them. Rebecca looked just the same, except she wasn't dressed in white and wasn't wearing a wreath of lilies in her hair. But the happy groom of the previous picture had been replaced by a grotesque mockery of humanity. It reminded me of a corpse I'd viewed at a murder scene, inflated by the build-up of gases after death. It had the bulk of the Michelin Man, but lacked his jolliness and extra-

terrestriality. Walter had become a golem, a monstrous parody of his former self. Now he had several chins, and his enormous stomach pressed tightly against the edge of the table. His face was swollen and grey in colour, and he didn't look at all healthy. He was frowning at the camera.

"How did he get like this?" I asked.

"She feeds him. All the time. Far too much, and everything that's bad for him. We stayed with them once – they've got a big house down in North Berwick – last year. He was already like this. I mean, David and I just have toast and coffee for breakfast, and so did Rebecca. But she made Walter the full Scottish – two fried eggs, two slices of square sausage, three pieces of streaky bacon, and two slices of black pudding. Oh, and a few mushrooms and a fried tomato. Then followed it up with a pile of pancakes smothered in maple syrup. And the toast came after that. And she was shovelling sugar into his tea as well. We couldn't believe it."

"He could easily say he doesn't want it. I'm guessing she's not forcing him to eat it."

"I got David to have a chat with him while we were out one day. He said Walter realises he's putting on weight but doesn't like to annoy Rebecca. She loves cooking for him, he says. I had a word with Rebecca too, but that didn't go well. She denied that Walter was overweight and asked what business it was of mine what she and Walter had to eat. She doesn't speak to me now. But there's something going on, I'm sure of it. She knows what she's doing. I think she's trying to make him so ill that he dies."

"What's she after, then?"

"Well, his money of course. He's not doing badly now, but he says he's making a bomb out of Brexit. Reckons it'll make him a millionaire twice over. She's got a motive there. Can the police do something?"

"Hmm. I'm not sure about that, Jackie. There would need to be proof that she's intending to kill him. Emails or witnesses to a conversation in which she makes that clear. Otherwise she's just overfeeding him, and that's not a crime. Especially if he's happy to be overfed. Unless, that is, she's done it before."

"What do you mean?"

"If that's really her intention, it may not be the first time. But even then, it would be very difficult to prove."

"Sally, could you find out? I mean, you've got databases and things. See if she's done it before. Please."

"Well, OK, I'll give it a shot. Don't tell anyone, especially not David. What's Rebecca's maiden name, and when did they get married? It shouldn't be too hard to look her up – I can do that tomorrow. And email me those photos. But don't expect any dramatic revelations. I really don't think there's anything we can do. Your best bet is to persuade Walter to put his foot down before it's too late."

Thankfully there was not much doing at the station on Thursday. DC Rankin was at his computer, so I asked him to check out Rebecca Chapman, working back from her wedding to Walter MacMahon in 2015.

Rankin's enthusiastic, and by lunchtime he'd got something for me. Rebecca Chapman was born in Dumfries in 1983. In 2006 she married a Jason Broadribb, with an address in Girvan. Broadribb died in 2009 of a heart attack. Two years later, in 2011, she'd married a Gerald Benchley at a Registry Office in Newcastle-on-Tyne. In 2013 the Benchleys were divorced. And two years later she was married again. According to Jackie her marriage to Walter took place at one of those spa hotels on the edge of Edinburgh. Rankin also supplied me with their ages at marriage: Jason Broadribb was fifty, twenty-seven years older than his bride; Gerald Benchley was fifty-two, twenty-four years older than Rebecca; and Walter was fifty-one, eighteen years older.

Three marriages to older men, the first two very short-lived, made me think this was worth looking into a bit more. But I'd have to okay it with the boss. Detective Chief Inspector Gillen was hard at work waxing his moustache when I came into his office. A little tin sat in front of him, the lid off, and a shiny substance visible within. Very few men could carry off the Kaiser Wilhelm look these days, and he wasn't one of them. However, he did manage to look like something out of a 1930s B-movie, and I don't mean Frankenstein. More like one of those men in dinner jackets hanging round the edge of the group when the murder is discovered in the country house, who turns out to be a swindler pretending to be a Hungarian Count.

"Sergeant McIsaac. Do take a seat. Nothing to do at present?"

"Following up a lead, sir, from a member of the public. Possible murder by overfeeding."

"I'm already sceptical. Tell me more."

I told him more. He wasn't convinced. He preferred deaths to be natural or, failing that, accidental. "If the chap won't stop eating, one can hardly blame his wife, eh?" Nevertheless, he gave me permission to spend a couple of days on it, mainly because there wasn't much doing, and it didn't look good if Fife's finest were sitting around with their feet up. Some councillor might start demanding we should all get back out on the beat. Gillen and I both knew that the chances of it leading to anything were negligible.

It didn't take long for Rankin to get me an address and phone number for Gerald Benchley. He was a self-employed accountant who worked from home, so I was able to talk to him right away. I arranged to see him the following day at 11.00 am. Then I phoned my colleagues in Girvan.

Just over two hours later I was parked outside the Girvan police station. The uniformed sergeant in charge – Sergeant Bruce – was happy to help. It was a welcome change from petty vandalism and dog shit on the pavements. He'd already sent an underling round to the library to consult the back numbers of the *Carrick Gazette*, and scan an article from February 2008. He put the sheet before me with a flourish. "How's that, Sergeant, nae flies on us, eh?"

I was duly impressed. The two hours I'd spent on the road had not been wasted here. "Sudden Death of Local Man," said the headline. Eyebrows raised rather than screaming. But it told me that Jason Broadribb had been a section manager at the gigantic distillery just outside the town, and a stalwart of the local golf club. In fact, according to the paper, he had collapsed on the fifteenth green, on the point of putting home for a three. Sergeant Bruce had already been in touch with the club, and got the name and address of a former committee member who, he was assured, knew Jason Broadribb well. I phoned him up and was invited over for 2 pm. That gave me time to grab a sandwich and a coffee at the cafe in the leisure centre by the harbour, and breath a little sea air.

Major Terence Blake (retd.) lived in a bungalow in a street of bungalows not far away from the sea-front. Once his wife had set out the coffee, he was happy to cast his still-sharp mind back.

"Oh yes," he said, "Jason was a good sort. Good player too. Handicap of…I forget now. We were all surprised when he told us he was getting married. Had him down as one of life's bachelors. And what a girl. Young enough to be his daughter, you know, and a good looker. We told him she'd be the death of him, you know, older man marries younger woman, got to be careful, eh? But I never saw it turning out the way it did. She was the death of him, all right." He paused for effect.

"How was that?" I was suitably keen to know.

"Fed him to death! God knows how he allowed her to do it. But he was besotted with her, she could do no wrong. We warned him, as soon as we saw him getting too heavy, well, obese is the word, I suppose. Doubled his weight in just two years. She didn't feed herself like that, oh no, just him. He loved chocolate. I mean, that's fine, as long as you don't overdo it. But she made it like Christmas every day. You know, when you used to get those selection boxes, Christmas was worth waiting for in those days."

"Do you think his wife realised she was feeding him too much?"

"Oh yes, no doubt about it. My wife spoke to her about it, didn't you, Bunty? Bunty used to be a nurse, knew what she was talking about, but the girl – what was her name…?"

"Rebecca," put in Mrs Blake.

"Yes, that was it, she was having none of it. Sent poor Bunty off with a flea in her ear. Nobody was telling her how to look after her man."

"What makes you so sure it was deliberate?"

"The way she looked at him, I mean, when he wasn't looking at her, and she didn't think anyone else was. Emotionless. Calculating. A few of us caught that look."

"What did she do after he died?"

"She got all his money, you know, somebody said it was over half a million, once she'd sold the house. Then she was off, vanished! No idea where she is now. Far away from here I hope."

I asked him if he had any photos of Jason and Rebecca. Bunty fetched an album and leafed through it. I borrowed one showing the couple not long before Jason's death. Remarkably similar to the picture Jackie had showed me. I thanked them and made my excuses.

Next morning was sunny and warm, a day full of promise. I was off early, across the bridge, and round the Edinburgh ring road onto the A1. The weather was dry, but still cold, a good day to travel. I didn't need to get tangled into Newcastle's urban sprawl, as Gerald Benchley lived in Ponteland, a wealthy-looking suburban reservation near the airport, north of the city. His house was large, detached, and neo-Georgian, with an ample garden paved over at the front to provide parking for his clients. A gleaming Porsche coupé was parked there; I guessed that was his. He'd opened the front door before I was out of the car. He was now sixty-one years old, if my arithmetic was right, and looked fit and well-tanned.

He waved. "Hi! Sergeant McIsaac. Come on in."

He ushered me into a spacious living-room with views onto an even more spacious back garden. As we sat down an attractive blonde came into the room from what I assumed was the kitchen. He introduced his wife; she was called Tracey and looked about twenty-two and very fit. She offered us coffee, then excused herself.

I came straight to the point, said I was looking into a case which involved his former wife, and I needed a bit of background. He was happy to talk. I'd already heard the story. He'd fallen head-over-heels for her, and they were married within months. She'd fed him up and within a couple of years he'd put on a vast amount of weight. But then the trajectory was interrupted. One of his clients, a surgeon who did private work on the side, told him quite bluntly that he'd have to look for a new accountant, as he reckoned Benchley would be dead within six months. That shook him up. Nothing talks like money! He started refusing the excess food Rebecca put before him, despite her pleas that it would just go to waste, and went to a gym. He took on a personal trainer, who put him on a demanding regime of diet and exercise. That led to a major argument with his wife, and one day he came home from the gym to discover Rebecca had left. Two weeks later she asked for a divorce. "She got two hundred and fifty grand at the settlement," he concluded, "but I got another thirty years of life! And my trainer's now my wife." He readily provided a photo of himself at his heaviest – "I keep it as a warning to myself. Stops me backsliding."

I hit the road north again, and decided to call in on Walter on the way back. I was lucky – he was in but Rebecca was out. He looked even worse than his picture. Once he'd lumbered over and lowered his enormous bulk into an armchair, which creaked in protest, I explained that I was looking into a case which involved a Jason Broadribb.

"I'm sorry," he said, "I don't recognise the name. What has this to do with me?"

"Jason Broadribb. Your wife's first husband."

"No. You must be mistaken. Her first husband was called Benchley. He treated her very badly, even hit her, so she divorced him."

"Ah," I said, trying to look understanding, "I'm sorry to have to correct you there, Mr. MacMahon. Your wife's first husband was in fact a Jason Broadribb. They married in 2006 in Girvan, and lived there, until Broadribb died in 2009. A heart attack. It was only two years after that that she married Mr. Benchley. I think you'll recognise your wife in this picture." I laid the photo of Jason and Rebecca on the coffee table in front of him. He picked it up and studied it, frowning, then put it down again. He said nothing.

I took out the picture of Gerald Benchley with Rebecca and put that alongside. "This is Mr Benchley with Rebecca," I explained. "She asked for the divorce when he decided to stop being over-fed. I should add that Mr. Benchley is still alive, and now a lot slimmer."

He stared at the two pictures for a long time. "Please explain why you're here, Sergeant McIsaac," he said hoarsely. He was trying to stay calm.

I'd have to float something plausible here. "Of course. We're looking into possible financial irregularities in relation to Mr Broadribb's estate. Tax avoidance, that sort of thing. Your wife inherited, I believe, something over half a million pounds."

Walter sat up, as much as he could. His eyes bulged out of his head. "Half a million!" he gasped. "I mean, I know about the fifty thousand she got from Benchley…"

"It was actually two hundred and fifty thousand, Mr MacMahon. I'm sorry, I assumed you'd be the person she'd ask to invest that much money wisely."

Walter said nothing. He picked up the two pictures again and stared at them with an intensity that I feared would set them alight. Then he started, as if he'd just noticed me there, shook his head, and handed them back to me. "As you know, my wife's not in at the moment." His voice was taut as wire. "Perhaps you could phone here another day and speak with her. The number's on my card." He took a card from a carved wooden box in the coffee table and passed it over.

"Could you tell me where she is at the moment?"

"She spends two days a week visiting her mother, who's in a care home near St. Andrews. She'll be back later this evening."

"You don't go with her?"

"The mother's demented apparently, my presence would only confuse her."

"That's a pity?"

"I've better things to do. Lot of work on. Brexit. People wanting to shift their investments."

I asked Walter where Rebecca was staying. He said she usually stayed in a B&B in Tayport, but he didn't know which one. He did, however, give me the name of the care home.

Next morning the weather was set fair again. I set off north, towards Dundee, leaving the main road just short of the Tay Bridge, and turning into Tayport, a pleasant little place with no pretensions. I'd half expected the care home to be fictitious, but it was real all right. So was Mrs Chapman, except that she'd died in 2012. Just two years after she'd arrived. I showed the receptionist a picture of Rebecca.

"Yes," she said, "that was the daughter. She arranged it all. Visited the old lady once a month. Very sweet but hard as nails underneath."

I asked if they still had an address for her. She looked it up for me. It looked like a flat, in Dundee.

"I know that block," said the receptionist. "Very des res. Near the airport, overlooking the river. You can't miss it."

I thanked her, and turned to go. I was finding the heat in there quite oppressive.

"Oh, just one other thing," said the receptionist. "You're the second person that's asked about Mrs Chapman. We had a phone call late yesterday afternoon. A man who said he was Mrs Chapman's nephew, wanted to know how she was. That's a bit odd, isn't it, you'd think he'd know she'd been gone a while. He asked for the daughter's address too, said his wife had lost it. But I didn't like the sound of him, so I said we no longer had it."

Des res was the correct term to apply to McGonagall Court, a modern but tasteful block four stories high, boasting three-bedroom apartments with generous balconies facing south over the river. Not cheap. Rebecca's confidential pied à terre was on the second floor. Was this where she stayed between marriages? There was no-one in.

Next morning I was sent up to DCI Gillen's lair as soon as I arrived at the station. He motioned me to sit down. "That woman you were looking into. Rebecca MacMahon?"

"Yes, that's her."

"Did you get very far?"

I gave him a run-down on what I'd done. "Something's up, isn't it?" I finally asked.

"You don't need to take that one any further, Sergeant. Your Mrs MacMahon's been found dead."

"But…How?"

"Don't worry, it seems to have been an accident. Looks like her husband – as you know, he's quite obese – rolled over onto her in bed in his sleep, and suffocated her. Never realised until he woke up later and found she wasn't responding. Called the emergency services right away, of course. Anyway, no need for us to be involved at all. North Berwick will handle it."

But I'd seen a hint of something in Walter's eye as he gazed at the photographs I'd shown him. "Look, sir," I said, "What we've got might suggest the death was not necessarily accidental. Between what I told Walter MacMahon, and what he may have found out himself, there could be a motive for murder."

He looked out the window at the tenement across the street. A sad young woman stood at the window opposite, holding a baby, then turned away.

"No," he said finally. "It's not our business, sergeant. There's nothing in what you say to make me think it's anything other than accidental. The man's a financial consultant, after all, goodness knows what it'll do to his business." He smiled a smile of satisfactory finality. "After all, maybe she was feeding him up. If so, it looks like she sowed the seeds of her own demise."

I was a Fugitive from a Care Home

I was writing up my report on the case of Elias Clembridge, when the call came in. He'd been selling fake season tickets for Hearts and Hibs to gullible Fifers, and was only caught out when the nice old gentleman he'd made his last sale to turned out to be a Hibs director. But this sounded a lot more interesting. Tracey at reception told me a man wanted to speak to a detective. "He says it's about a murder," she said.

"That would be me," I said. "Put him on the line."

The voice on the line was male, and was little more than a whisper. "My name," it said, "is Roddy Struthers."

"Detective Sergeant McIsaac. How can I help you?"

"Remember the death at the Last Horizon? 2012."

"The name rings a bell. I wasn't on that case, so I don't know the details."

"I can give you them. Come and see me. I need to tell someone."

"Where are you, Mr Struthers?" He gave me an address in Ayr.

I glanced at my watch. 12.30 pm. Too late to go over today. "Would tomorrow morning be OK?"

"Aye, that would be just grand. It'll be a weight off my mind."

"I'll be there about ten."

The Clembridge report could wait. That would give me time to dig out the file on the Last Horizon, and familiarise myself with it. It took a while to sift through it, but I was able to form a pretty clear account of what had happened.

The Last Horizon Care Home was located just off the A955 between Kirkcaldy and East Wemyss. The brochure in the file described it as having 'a stunning view of the Firth of Forth.' However, a police photograph showed that the only person who would enjoy this view would be the man who came to scrape the moss off the roof tiles. For the residents, the view was mainly of the housing estate which Farewell Developments had built on two thirds of the land they had acquired for the care home. The 'extensive gardens' they advertised in the brochure had never materialised, and the 'acres of natural woodland' were soon bulldozed for the houses.

On the sign at the entrance to the care home area, some graffiti artist had over-written the words 'Last Horizon' with 'Final Solution.' Farewell Developments plc took its profit-making aims very seriously, more so than the comfort of its residents, described in internal company documents as 'human throughput commodity.' The company also managed private prisons, and found the same principles applied to both types of institution. You just had to pretend the care home was not a prison. And you could pay the staff a lot less.

Police were called on the morning of Thursday 22 March, 2012. It was reported that a member of staff had been found dead. Uniformed officers who headed there from Glenrothes found, in one of the bedrooms, the body of Simeon Bulliver, aged 37. CID were immediately called in, and I must admit I had to smile when I read that the Senior Investigating Officer was none other than my current boss, Detective Chief Inspector Gillen. That must have been quite soon after his promotion to DI.

Back to the story. Bulliver was one of two staff responsible for overnight supervision of the home, which housed 48 elderly people. On the night of the 21st, however, his colleague, Daphne Wilmer, was obliged to go home not long after midnight, feeling unwell, leaving Bulliver in sole charge. At 6.55 the following morning two staff members arrived to take over supervision duties.

The two supervisory staff – I hesitate to call them 'nurses' as they had no nursing qualifications – noticed that Bulliver was not at the reception desk, where he would normally have been to do the morning handover. Wilmer had however recorded her departure in the log book. Nor was Bulliver in the night station, half way down the main corridor on the ground floor. Some of the residents were already moving about, but they either knew nothing of his whereabouts or were not coherent in their responses to the staff's enquiries.

Eventually they decided to search the whole place, in case he'd been taken ill, and collapsed somewhere. They soon discovered he was not in any of the public areas, and proceeded to check the bedrooms. When they reached Room 124, on the first floor, the occupant, Alistair Grantully, aged 85, was in the room, and denied having seen Bulliver. Grantully was suffering from dementia, and may not even have known who Bulliver was. However, the next room, number 125, was in a strange state. The wardrobe, which stood against the wall opposite the bed, had been moved a little, a crystal flower vase, which was normally on the window ledge of number 124, was lying on the carpet, with what looked like a bloodstain around it. The bed looked as if it had not been slept in, and the occupant of the room, Roderick Struthers, aged 74, was not there.

They assumed that Struthers had had an accident, and that Bulliver had moved him somewhere. However, by the time they'd completed the search of the rooms it was evident that both Bulliver and Struthers were missing. It was then observed that Bulliver's car, a black Mercedes A180 Sport, was not in the car park. Perhaps, they thought, Bulliver had had to take Struthers to hospital. Since Wilmer said that Bulliver was present when she left, and that nothing untoward had happened until then, this must have occurred after her departure. That would be contrary to the rules, which stated clearly that the building must not be left unattended; the correct response to any serious injury was to dial 999 and call an ambulance. However, as one of them admitted, Bulliver did not always adhere to the rules. So they phoned the local hospital, only to discover that neither Bulliver nor Struthers were there.

This was puzzling, but the normal life of the institution had to continue, so they put the matter to one side, hoping that the missing pair would soon turn up, and focused on getting all the residents processed through breakfast. 'Processed' was the word used in their statements, and indeed, the operating procedures for the home issued by Farewell Developments prescribe the day as a series of processes, through which all residents must be put. These included getting up, washing, breakfast, passing of bowels, medications, leisure, lunch, and so on, and each resident was ticked off as each 'waymark' was passed.

After breakfast the residents were shepherded into the lounge areas – there were two, one at each end of the building – so that the rooms could be cleaned and tidied. During this process, the rooms were also checked by the cleaning staff for prohibited items. These included bottles of alcohol, magazines or books of an 'unsuitable' nature, and food items such as chocolate, marzipan, etc. Regular checking was necessary as visitors often brought these items in without reference to the staff.

Cleaning proceeded normally until it reached room 124. The cleaner noticed, on tidying Mr Grantully's bed, that there was something bulky stowed beneath it. She pulled it out with some difficulty and discovered, wrapped in the spare blanket usually kept in the wardrobe, the body of Simeon Bulliver. She at once reported this to the supervisory staff, who called the police.

DI Gillen, on arrival, was led to Room 124, where he observed Bulliver's body. The body was clad in the usual care home attire: lightweight top and trousers in light blue, and moccasins. It was clear he was dead. His head had suffered severe injuries – in plain language it had been bashed in. An obvious case of murder.

Other residents were questioned, but none could throw any light on the matter. Most said they'd been asleep, three added that they were also deaf, and wouldn't have heard anything anyway. Several had no idea what the police interviewers were talking about, and one confessed to stealing a stick of rock from a souvenir shop in Blackpool in 1966.

No-one, either staff or residents, expressed any sorrow that Bulliver was dead. The staff said they hardly knew him, and he kept himself to himself. The residents, to a man and woman, said they knew nothing about him. The interviewer got the distinct impression that they didn't like him. I should add that I didn't blame them. Bulliver, it emerged, had a police record for drug offences and assault. Even his photograph was intimidating.

I should remind you here that Gillen, whom I've worked with for a number of years, believes firmly that the simplest and most obvious solution is always correct. Taking this approach results in good clear-up times for cases, and a minimum of additional resource requirement, and gets Gillen plenty of brownie points with the high-ups. Occasionally, of course, it results either in a case that collapses, or an act of injustice. If the former, the prosecution service flags that there's no case, and the investigation is quietly put on the shelf. If the latter, somebody does time for something he didn't do.

The obvious solution here was that Grantully or Struthers, or both, had killed Bulliver, then hidden the body under Grantully's bed. When questioned however, Grantully immediately confessed to the killing, saying he had hit 'the bad man' over the head repeatedly with a flower vase. When asked about Struthers, he expressed no knowledge of who Struthers was. When asked simply about the man in the next room, he said that next door was his spare room, that he had found the bad man in his spare room and had dealt with him. He expressed satisfaction that the bad man was dead. When asked why he had killed Bulliver, he said he'd stolen his milk when he was at school, and he also knew he was the man who shot JR Ewing. He went on to allege that the dead man was his evil twin who, after a life of depravity in the colonies, had come back to steal his soul. After an examination by psychologists, it was concluded that Grantully was unfit to plead, and with the agreement of the procurator fiscal, Gillen declared the case closed.

The fact remained however, that Struthers had vanished, as well as Bulliver's car, clothes and wallet. Gillen concluded that Struthers had taken advantage of Grantully's killing of Bulliver to steal his effects and 'abscond' with Bulliver's car. Struthers' details were circulated, but nothing came back. It was discovered that £2,000 had been taken from cash machines in Kirkcaldy, using Bulliver's credit and debit cards, on the night of the killing, and one of the cards had been used to buy items at a supermarket near Dunfermline. The cards had not been used again, and were cancelled two days after the discovery of Bulliver's body, when the police contacted the banks. There had been no trace of Struthers since.

As for the car, it was eventually located four years later, when a speeding driver was apprehended on the M8. The driver, Roy Connor, aged 32, claimed he had bought it in good faith from a man he'd met at the sheep market in Selkirk, whose name and appearance he couldn't remember. The car had false registration plates and had no MOT certificate. Connor expressed bafflement over these facts, swearing the man in Selkirk had assured him everything was in order. As for the facts that he had no motor insurance and had not paid the road tax, he explained that he had been living in Ireland for many years and was ignorant of how these things were done. He also claimed he was being harassed because he was dyslexic. The car was eventually identified from the engine and chassis numbers as being that originally owned by Bulliver.

So it was now nearly ten years since the death of Bulliver, and now, out of the blue, a man claiming to be Roderick Struthers had contacted us. I was keen to see what he could add to the details we already possessed. I debated whether to share this information with Chief Inspector Gillen, but in the end decided there would be no point. He would no doubt be averse to the case being opened up again, if that turned out to be necessary, since it might reflect badly upon himself. I knew that Gillen was, in any case, away tomorrow, on a course about 'unconscious bias' in policing, so there was no chance he would suddenly ask me to do something.

So, at eight o'clock the following morning I was on the road west. I made good progress and by 9.45 was in a quiet road, with bungalows on both sides, not far from the beach on the south side of Ayr. I parked outside number 64, and by the time I'd got out, an elderly woman was waiting in the doorway.

"Come away in," she called. "It's awfy chilly out here."

It was extremely warm inside. She took my jacket, the one with the thick fleece lining I wear on wintry days, and hung it on an ancient coat-stand in the hall, then pointed me to the living room.

"I'm Glenda, Glenda Lockhart. I'll just be making a pot of tea. You go in. I've already heard it all. I just hope he's doin the right thing. But he needs to get it off his chest, so he does."

The living room was even warmer than the hallway. The gas fire was on to augment the central heating. Two comfy armchairs flanked the fire, and in one of them sat an old man. Thankfully not in the last stages of decrepitude, I reckoned he'd once been a fine figure of a man, now rather more gaunt and grey than once he'd been. He pushed himself up with some difficulty from the chair to shake hands. I guessed he'd be well over eighty.

"Sergeant McIsaac?" I nodded. "I'm so glad you've come. Take a wee seat there now."

He pointed to the other chair. I sat down. He began to talk right away. Here's his story, as he told it. I've edited out the bits where I express interest, etc. and ask him to go on.

If you ask any of the neighbours who lives here, they'll tell you it's George Lockhart. But I've only been him since 2012. My real name is Roderick Struthers. I used to have my own company. We supplied mobility equipment, all over the country, even down into England. It was a growing market, and I didn't do too badly. I sold the business off in 2005 when I was 65. I had a good pension and a nice house. I'd been divorced a good few years then. See, I was away a lot and Margie never got used to that. So she, well, that doesn't matter now. I was on my own, that's the point.

It was the autumn of 2011 when I got ill. I don't know what it was, the doctors didn't either, they thought it was some sort of virus, but it weakened the immune system, so various bacteria got in, and caused some havoc. See, I woke up one day and didn't know who I was. I went to the front door and collapsed on the doorstep. I woke up four days later in hospital. I was delirious for another week. And exhausted for another two. They said I'd had pneumonia, with complications. The pills they gave me made me light-headed, so when they told me I could go home, and the car was waiting, I just got in. My younger sister, Betty, was there. It was her husband Eric's car, a big one. He's an accountant, by the way, they live in Haddington. He was driving. I didn't recognise where we were going. She said, 'It's just somewhere to stay till you get better. Where you can be properly looked after.'

That's how I arrived at The Last Horizon. I was still far from well, so for a couple of months I just went with the flow. It was quite nice not having to decide anything. OK, the food wasn't that great, but it was there three times a day, and even a cup of tea and a biscuit before bed-time. But there comes a point when you want to get on with your life. I'd tried to contact Betty several times with no success. I didn't have a phone – that didn't seem to have come with me to the hospital. I wrote letters, but now I'm not sure if the people there even posted them.

Eventually I got a letter from some lawyers in Edinburgh, writing on behalf on my sister. They informed me that during my stay in hospital – presumably when I was *non compos mentis* – I'd signed a power of attorney for her. Since doctors had advised I would probably need a care regimen for the rest of my life, she had then sold my house and car, and used part of the proceeds to buy me a lifetime residence at The Last Horizon. The lawyers informed me they possessed signed affidavits from two doctors and a psychologist approving this course of action. There was no mention of what happened to the rest of the money. The house had been cleared and all my possessions sold off or otherwise disposed of. It was made clear that any attempt to contest this 'settlement of your affairs' would be met with rigorous legal action.

So that was me stuck in The Last Horizon. After getting the letter, I thought I'd make a break for it, maybe visit my bank and a lawyer. I soon discovered I had no money, no credit or debit card, no car key, no driving licence, in fact no ID of any sort. I'd got used to walking around the place in slippers, but when I looked for my shoes, I found they were gone too. My wardrobe contained no outdoor garment of any sort. When I asked at reception, they said I didn't need them for the moment, as the doctor had said I was not be permitted to go out, 'in the interests of my health.' I was, in effect, a prisoner.

I resolved to wait until an opportunity to escape presented itself. In the meantime I tried to look as if I'd accepted my fate. I got to know the other residents. The man next door, Grantully, was, I have to say, bonkers. His dementia level varied from day to day. Some days he was almost sane, others he was completely away with the fairies. I got on well with some of the female residents. Some were of course gaga, but others had, rather like me, been simply dumped there by their families at the earliest opportunity.

As they got to know and trust me, I began to hear things, not very nice things, about what went on in the home during the night. Mainly concerning Bulliver. While some of the staff were dedicated and genuinely helpful people, others were prone to minor pilfering of residents' property or simply dealing with them as if they were animals. Bulliver was on a different plane. One very respectable lady who finally decided to confide in me told me of his nocturnal visits to those who still retained anything like a female body, and the pleasures he took in sexually abusing them.

Others confirmed her story. They'd tried to complain to the other staff but no-one seemed willing to listen. One lady who was persistent in her complaints was visited by Bulliver one night and beaten up. When she was found in the morning she could not speak, and she remained silent until she died six weeks later. No action was taken over that matter. One carer told me the staff had been ordered by Farewell Developments to ignore any complaints, since any whiff of unease would damage the place's profitability.

Eventually I had a bit of a run-in with Bulliver myself. I don't always sleep easily and one night about one a.m. I was heading for the lounge to stretch my legs a bit, when I heard groans and laughter from Room 103, at the other end of my floor. I opened the door to find Bulliver...well, I'm not going to say what he was doing to poor Dorothy Bryant, but I told him to stop at once. He told me to fuck off or he'd kick my head in. He was a big man, and always had a nasty look about him, so I said OK and left. But as soon as I reached the staircase, I set off the fire alarm. It was one of those ones where you smash the glass and press the red button. Bulliver had to stop what he was doing and shepherd everybody out. The fire brigade soon arrived and he had to deal with them too. That might have given me an opportunity to escape, but I still had no shoes. Besides which, I had a purpose now. I wanted to kill Bulliver.

My plan was soon made. I knew he'd have guessed it was me who'd set off the alarm, and would come during the next few nights to get his revenge. My aim was simple: to trap him in my room and deal with him somehow. I rigged a trip wire, made from my dressing gown cord, stretching from the bed frame across to the armchair, and about four inches off the floor. Then I put all the heavy stuff I could find – books mainly, I had a good few of them – into the top shelf of the wardrobe and took everything else out, so that it was nice and top-heavy. I moved it a couple of inches away from the wall, so that I could get my hand round the back at the top. The plan was that he would trip on the cord, then I'd push the wardrobe over on top of him. Then I planned to untie the cord and use it to strangle him. I would then make my escape.

I didn't have long to wait. He turned up the very next night after the alarm. Instead of lying in bed, I sat in the armchair. I must have dozed a bit, but sometime in the night I heard the door handle turn. He swung the door open, with no attempt at stealth – he had the building to himself after all – and barged in, switching the light on as he came. But he had to grope for the switch and once he'd found it his foot was already under the cord. The light came on and at the same time he fell forwards, exactly as planned. So far so good.

I jumped to my feet and heaved the wardrobe over. It teetered, then fell. Unfortunately I hadn't quite calculated the distances and the top of it hit the side of the bed frame and lodged there, so he didn't get the full force of it on him. I couldn't get round the wardrobe to him, and he began to crawl out, shouting that he was going to fucking kill me. He got out from under the wardrobe, stood up – he was six inches taller than me – and leaning down, flipped up the wardrobe as if it were made of balsa wood. He looked at me and smiled.

Now he noticed the door was still open. He gave me a shove that threw me down into the armchair, and went past me to shut it. He was still shouting at me as he grasped the door handle. Then I heard a thump and a gasp. Grantully was standing in the doorway holding a large crystal vase, which he'd used to hit Bulliver on the head. Bulliver staggered back, his heel caught on the cord, which was still in place, and he fell backwards onto the floor. Grantully marched into the room, stepping neatly over the cord, and smashed the vase onto Bulliver's face. Then he knelt down on his chest and repeatedly bashed the vase into his face, until there wasn't a face there any more. Then he tried to get up, and I had to give him a hand.

'Bad man finished,' he simply said. 'We take him next door.'

Together we dragged Bulliver's body through to Grantully's room, then wrapped him in a spare blanket and rolled him under the bed. Then Grantully said to me, 'Now you go.' Those three sentences were the only words he ever spoke to me.

I didn't wait for further encouragement. This was my only chance to get out of there, and now that Bulliver was dead, I could do it without feeling I was deserting the others.

I knew exactly what to do. I headed straight for the night station. It wasn't locked. Inside, in a locker, were Bulliver's clothes and shoes. I took off my dressing gown and put them on. The shirt and jacket were a bit long, but who would notice? The shoes were a bit big, but they'd do well enough. I'd kept my own socks on, just in case tonight was the night. In the locker I also found his wallet and car keys. In the wallet were several debit and credit cards, and £480 in cash. That would come in useful.

I brought my dressing gown and slippers with me, and exited the building via the kitchen. I guessed the rear door would be unlocked. I'd seen Bulliver out there smoking before. In the car park there was only one car, a rather nice black Mercedes, and his key opened it. It smelt new inside. I checked the glove compartment; there was the car's registration form, a bundle containing £5,500 rolled in an elastic band and a small packet of white powder. In two minutes the engine was purring and I followed the drive, and then turned left onto the A955 to head west.

It was only now that I saw from the clock in the car that it was 2.20 am. My first stop was Kirkcaldy. There were no cars parked by the cash machine at the bank. I put the first debit card in, and waited to be asked for a PIN. I had only one shot on this. I'd noted on his driving licence that he was born in 1975, so I keyed in those four numbers. It worked! He had five cards altogether, all of which accepted the same PIN, so I left the cash machine £2,000 richer. I now had £7,980, which I hoped would keep me going for a while.

Half an hour later, near Dunfermline, I came across a large

24-hour supermarket. Time for a final splurge with Bulliver's cards. I suspected they'd be cancelled by the morrow, and even if I tried to use them again, it would only pinpoint my location. I bought some sandwiches, a bottle of good whisky, a rucksack, a couple of shirts and pairs of trousers– the choice was very limited – a fleece, a waterproof jacket, a couple of CDs – I didn't want to listen to reggae for the rest of the night – and a laptop, the most expensive they had. There was a card-only self-service fuel station too, so I filled up the car. There was a drain grating near the pump, so I popped the cards through and heard a satisfying little splash below. Into a rubbish bin nearby went my dressing gown and slippers, and the little bag of white powder. I didn't know what it was, but didn't want it in the car if it were stopped.

Now for the long drive. I needed to be a good way away by the morning, and preferably out of Scotland. I was soon across the Forth Bridge and round the Edinburgh Ring Road to pick up the A68 south. I wanted to avoid the motorways; that was where the first cameras they'd check would be. I crossed the border at Carter Bar and followed the A68 right down to the junction near Darlington where it joined the A1, then kept on going till I reached Doncaster.

I must admit I could have driven that car for ever, it was so smooth, but I had other plans for it. I drove into Doncaster, then pulled into a layby and slept for a few hours. By eight I was on the road again. After inquiring at a cafe and a newsagent, I found what I was looking for, a big sign saying, 'We buy any car for cash.' I knew the Merc must have cost Bulliver around thirty grand, but I certainly wouldn't get anything near it. At least with the papers, it would be a legal sale. I could easily forge Bulliver's scrawling signature. We argued for a while, and in the end he gave me fifteen thousand, plus an eight-year-old grey Astra with 100,000 miles on the clock. That took my kitty up to just over twenty-one thousand, and I had some less noticeable wheels.

Now I drove west across country, below Manchester and Liverpool, and into North Wales. I needed a place I could disappear in, so I made for Llandudno, and checked into a modest B&B without a sea view under the name George

Lockhart. That was a stroke of luck. It was run by a widow name of Glenda Jones. Yes, you met her when you arrived. She was from Ayrshire, but had married a Welshman years before, and moved to Llandudno where they'd run the B&B until he died, that was in 2008, I think. So it was like a breath of fresh air, having a Scot as a long-term lodger.

We got very well with each other, so well that she eventually asked me to move in with her and help run the place. I didn't want her to be under any illusions about me, so at that point I told her the whole story. Thankfully it didn't make any difference. And I remained George Lockhart. Now I had a permanent address, so I could open a bank account and gradually feed my kitty into it.

Even in Llandudno, the papers reported Bulliver's death. But luckily the only photos they printed were of Bulliver, and they revelled in his criminal record. Grantully's confession was reported, and they mentioned in passing that another resident of the home seemed to have taken advantage of the event to steal Bulliver's car and make off. I wasn't named, and there was no picture of me.

After her husband had died Glenda had begun to think of returning to Scotland. But we waited three years, until I thought the business at the care home would be forgotten. Then we sold up the B&B and moved up here. And we've been here ever since. Of course, I don't have a National Insurance number, so I don't get a pension. But we manage, and it's not expensive here. The doctors were a bit iffy when I tried to sign up, but I said I'd been in South Africa for a long time, and the paperwork would eventually come through, so they gave me a temporary ID number.

Why did I call you? Well, I'm eighty-four now. I don't feel too bad at the moment, but you know how it is, at any moment something can come up. And I've always wanted to put my side of the story. Not necessarily to become Roddy Struthers again, but just to know that it's been told.

"They'll no put him in jail, will they?" asked Glenda, who'd come into the room soon after we started talking. "He's far too old for that."

"You're never too old to be put in jail," I replied, "but only if your crime is a really bad one. Like mass murder, or being a concentration camp guard. I don't think a car theft eight years ago comes anywhere near that bracket. And considering what Bulliver had been up to, I suspect the most you'll get is a telling-off from the sheriff, and a warning not to do it again. Let me see what I can do."

The next day I spoke to the procurator fiscal, who said any attempt to pursue the theft case would be a waste of time and money, and it should be left closed. She also suggested that I add a note to the case files reporting the facts as Mr Struthers had told me. DCI Gillen was happy with that outcome too. His conclusion about the killing was not under any question, but he felt there would be no point in dredging it all up again. "And I have to say," he pontificated, "Struthers' evidence does show us that fellow Bulliver had it coming. Got what he deserved, in my opinion."

At the weekend I revisited the Lockharts to let them know the good news. I'd also spoken to the DWP, and it seemed that Roddy Struthers was entitled to all the pension money he'd not received since he'd entered The Last Horizon. They considered prosecuting his sister, but discovered that she was herself now a resident of The Last Horizon, and had been unable to understand any of the questions she was asked.

I finally asked Roddy/George what he wanted to do about his name.

"It would simply confuse the neighbours if I suddenly became someone else. So I'll change my name by deed poll to George Lockhart, and I'll still have all the rest of Roddy's identity. But I've now got a great story I can tell at the Bowling Club. It'll keep me in drinks for months!"

Tales of Assassins

Seen but for a Moment

Ross Tearlaw watched the snow whirling past his carriage window and disappearing into the darkness. He sat in a three-carriage train of rather old rolling stock, which had left Gourock at 16.08 and should arrive at Glasgow Central at 16.49, if it weren't delayed by the weather. He spent most of the journey going over the notes he'd made at his meeting with the client. At 16.46 he put his notebook away, zipped up his jacket, and put on his woolly hat and insulated gloves.

The train crossed the Clyde and passed the stone piers at the entrance to Central Station, only five minutes late. As it slowed to a halt he saw a train on the very next line, already full, and about to leave. He was just getting to his feet, when the departing train set off. Distracted by the movement, he glanced round, and for a fleeting moment, as the carriage pulled past, he saw the face of a man sitting at the window opposite him. The face imprinted itself on his memory, for he knew it. But from where?

As his homeward train, the 17.01 to East Kilbride, rumbled through the darkness, he racked his brain for a fix on that face. By the time he got off at Clarkston he thought he had it. It was a face he hadn't seen for a long time, and he needed to be sure. But as a professional genealogist, finding people was Ross's business.

He reached his home, a 1930s-built bungalow, greeted his wife, and made for his study in the attic. It didn't take long on www.meetyouroldschoolpals.com to find a section devoted to his old school. Someone had put up photos of classes from 30 years ago. And there he saw the face, a lot younger but still recognisable. The thin face and delicate nose, and the red scar visible on the forehead. But in the photo the eyes were downcast, whereas the man on the train had, for that fraction of time, looked straight at him. The names were along the bottom of the picture, and there it was: Marcus Laxtoun.

Now he remembered. As a senior pupil, one lunch break he'd

come across three boys taunting a frightened Laxtoun, then in his first year. He warned off the three, and after that kept a lookout for the younger boy. He'd noticed the red scar on the right side of his forehead. Laxtoun told him he'd slipped in his garden and cut his head on a piece of corrugated iron. Ross didn't believe him, but let it go. A year and a half later he left the school for university, and put away all memory of his schooldays.

He put Laxtoun's name into several search engines, but apart from the link to the picture he'd just seen, they came up with nothing.

As usual, the bullies had a leader, and in another photo, a class a year older than Laxtoun's, he found him: Rodney Kreetch. Large and overfed, probably pampered at home, grinning smugly at the camera. This time there were more links, the majority to newspapers in the North of England five years previously. Kreetch had become an estate agent, based in Harrogate, a well-heeled spa town in Yorkshire. One afternoon he'd driven to a house just outside the town, for sale at offers over £2.5 million, to meet a client, a Doctor McLeod. When he failed to come into his office the next morning, and calls to his home were not answered, two of his employees went to the house he'd gone to the previous day and found his body, in an armchair in the spacious living-room, shot twice in the chest. His Porsche coupé was found two days later by police in the car park off the Eastbound lane of the M8 at Harthill Services.

The main suspect was naturally Dr. McLeod. The staff at the estate agents' office could describe him, as he'd come in person to make the appointment. And a taxi-driver had taken him out to the fateful house. Many efforts were made, but despite a photofit Dr. McLeod was never found. Police suggested he'd killed Kreetch, driven his car to Harthill, and taken a bus to Edinburgh or Glasgow. He could therefore already have been out of the country by the time the crime was discovered.

The photofit picture could have been anybody with a fairly thin face and a beard, but when Ross drew the scar on a printout, and put a finger over the chin to hide the beard, the resemblance sprang out of the image at him. Marcus Laxtoun gazed expressionlessly at him from the paper.

But Ross doubted his discovery. Had Laxtoun killed Kreetch five years ago, and today sat in a train in Glasgow? This was surely nonsense. Tricks played by the mind. His brain had probably made up for the incomplete image it had of the man in the train by finding one in deep memory that vaguely fitted. And the photofit, although it might be Laxtoun, could easily be a thousand others. He put the matter aside and went downstairs to see what was for tea.

The next afternoon he was working at his laptop, tracing the client's family in Gourock back to a Greenock tenement, and before that to a croft on Mull. There was no-one else in the house, his wife being at South Glasgow College running a weaving workshop, so when the doorbell rang he answered it himself.

Time stopped. It was the man he had seen on the train! Ross could only stare at him.

"May I come in?" said he quietly. "I won't keep you long." He spoke without any accent, and his face was as impassive as his photofit likeness.

Ross found his voice. "Er, yes, of course. I'm making coffee." He led the man to the kitchen, and invited him to sit at the table. The man had brought in a canvas shopping bag, and as he sat, laid it carefully on the floor by his chair. There was evidently something heavy in it. He was wearing a waterproof jacket over a dark-coloured fleece, and dark blue chinos. And gloves, close-fitting and of some fabric Ross could not identify. His fair hair was cut short, and Ross noticed that the scar was not there. Was this perhaps not Laxtoun after all? It didn't feel good.

"Yes," said the man, "I had the scar treated, some time ago."

"Laxtoun?"

He smiled thinly. "I'm afraid I haven't been Marcus Laxtoun for quite a few years now. It wasn't a very helpful kind of name. You recognised me on the train, didn't you, Ross? I had to assume you would. That's why I came round for a chat."

"How did you find me?" gasped Ross. He groped for normality. "Er, care for some coffee? I was just about to make it."

"Thank you, but no thanks. Feel free to make some for

yourself. Finding you wasn't hard, Ross. You're a genealogist, your job is to find people, mainly dead people, and, as it were, bring them to life. Mine is, I guess, somewhat similar, except that I do it the other way round. Here's my card." He took from his jacket pocket a small metal case, opened it, extracted a card, and laid it on the table.

Ross read it: 'Gregor Castellan, Locational Solutions, Inc.' There was a website and an email address, both ending in .com. He put the card down on the counter. The kettle had boiled and he reached for the jar of coffee. His hands were shaking, and half his spoonful of coffee missed the mug. He hastily added the water from the kettle. His hand shook as he added the milk and he splashed in too much, so that it sloshed over the rim of the mug onto the counter. He wiped the counter with a dish towel, then, trying to avoid shaking, carefully set the mug on the table and sat down opposite Castellan.

"You seem very nervous, Ross, so I'm guessing there's a bit more, isn't there?" His voice was quiet, but hard, and he looked into Ross's eyes, without expression.

Ross felt Castellan's gaze inside his head. He opened his mouth, but nothing came out.

"I thought so," Castellan went on. "You're not stupid. So now, Ross, you and I share a little secret, don't we? Quite a dangerous little secret."

"Kreetch?" whispered Ross.

"Being bullied is very damaging," said Castellan, as if he hadn't heard the question. "To the mind more than to the body. It took me many years, and some tough experiences, to exorcise the self-image that Kreetch created for me. To recover my own self, find who I really was. But I did it, eventually. And I made a list of goals for my life. Near the bottom of the list I put 'Kill Kreetch.' Do you think people can change over time, Ross?"

Ross took a swig of the coffee. It was too hot and he burnt his tongue. He put the mug down hastily, spilt a little more, wiped it with his handkerchief. He wasn't sure what answer was required. "Yes, I suppose so."

With the back of his gloved hand, Castellan swept the mug

of coffee off the edge of the table, and it smashed on the floor. "Not good enough, Ross!" His voice a cold snarl. "Don't ever suppose when you talk to me. Tell me exactly what you think. Now!"

Ross felt something tighten in the pit of his stomach. His brain was paralysed. The only thing he could say was what was obvious. "You're different from the boy I knew then."

Castellan was silent for a moment, and he looked past Ross, as if someone stood in the doorway. "Yes," he said, as if talking to the newcomer, "that's true enough. But it was far from easy. So many people, especially men, gain such satisfaction from exerting power over others, that they can't see what they are themselves. They define their victims, but also themselves." His gaze recovered its stony edge, and raked over Ross's face.

Ross forced himself to speak. "I understand you."

Castellan nodded. "Good. That's why I allowed Kreetch that opportunity too. I gave him time, plenty of it, to understand what he was, and to repent of it. Yes, I know that's a religious sort of way to put it, but the word conveys, as no other, that someone really understands and takes responsibility for the things they've done. If Kreetch had achieved this, I'd have forgiven him. If not, well, it would be the other option."

"And he hadn't?"

"I'd been abroad a long time. Eventually I came back here to find him. It wasn't hard, people like him are never discreet. Even the few things I read told me he hadn't changed, but I needed to confirm it. That's why I went to his office – I waited till he'd gone out, of course – and as soon as I mentioned his name to the woman at the desk, I could tell from her reaction that he was the same old Kreetch. So I arranged to meet him at the house the following morning. What happened next, Ross? You tell me."

Ross could feel cold sweat on his forehead, and round his neck. But he had to think, to humour this stranger who was not the fearful boy he'd known. Now it was he who felt the junior, the weakling. He struggled to think. "You took a taxi to the house. You met him there. Didn't he recognise you?"

"No," said Castellan, smiling to himself, "he didn't. Of course, I'd lost the scar by then. I pretended to be unfamiliar with the housing market, willing to be led. He sensed a chance to make a killing, if I can use an unfortunate expression. He became expansive, told jokes. He was trying to press me into making an offer right away, kept talking about another client who was keen, so I'd have to move quickly. What a fool! He sat down in one of the armchairs, to discuss a deal. Then I shot him."

Despite his fear, Ross was puzzled. "Didn't you confront him with what he'd done. Tell him why you were killing him. Remind him who you were."

"Yes, that's what happens in books, isn't it? But my object was simply to kill him. If I'd made a drama out of it, I'd be making myself like him. I derived satisfaction, maybe even relief, from his death. But not pleasure."

"And then you drove his car to the service station, got the next bus to Edinburgh Airport, flew to Amsterdam perhaps. Then on somewhere else. And shaved off the beard."

"That's not bad. I knew you were clever." Castellan smiled thinly again

Ross felt he had to keep Castellan talking. "So why did you come back?"

"I had some business here, that's all. I was on my way to the airport when we caught sight of each other."

"So you had to change your plans?"

"I recognised you at once and knew you weren't daft. I suspected you'd put two and two together, and needed to be sure what you'd do with the answer. That's why I'm here."

Ross tried to swallow, but found he couldn't. "What are you going to do?" he croaked.

"I don't kill people without good reason, Ross. But if I have to, then...By the way, you've a lovely wife, you know. Louise, isn't it? She's very well thought of by her colleagues at the College, I discovered. And I sat in on a lecture your daughter gave at the University this morning – on the poetry of Elizabeth Melville – most interesting. We had a nice chat afterwards. I'm sure you're proud of her. It's tough to lose people you love, isn't it? And you don't know what complications might arise if you took what you know to the police. They might even accuse you of being complicit. They'll be keen to pin it on somebody."

Ross felt the cold run through him. He shivered. "I'll say nothing," he whispered.

"Good. I thought I could trust you. Just remember that if you do talk, I'll always find out." He paused, and smiled again. "But there's another reason I came round. Something that was also on my list."

Ross froze. It was like so many novels. Something very bad right at the end, just when you thought it was safe to go outside. He glanced at the knife handles protruding from the block on the counter. Could he grab one?

"Please, Ross, no dramatics. One, you don't know how to use a knife. And two, you see these gloves. My hands are important to my work, so I protect them. Woven into the material are links of titanium steel wire, a bit like mini-chain-mail. I can take hold of a knife by the blade, without injury. Neat, eh?"

Ross felt himself succumb to a paralysis of the mind, a state of limbo.

Castellan lifted the canvas bag onto his knees. "You see, Ross," he went on, "I never got the chance to thank you for helping me, all those years ago. It was you who started me on the path to resisting Keetch and becoming what I am now."

He groped in the canvas bag and Ross held his breath.

Out came a dark wooden box, about fifteen inches long, four wide and four deep.

"This is for you, Ross. It's a 45-year-old Lagavulin. You do like whisky, don't you?"

Ross looked at Castellan, and for a second, in his eyes, he saw the boy in the playground all those years ago, freed from those who sought to make him someone else.

Castellan had a modest hire car parked outside, and Ross watched as he drove off.

Ross Tearlaw was skilled at finding people. But he could find no trace of Gregor Castellan or Locational Solutions Inc., and the internet and the email addresses only delivered error messages.

The View from the Balcony

Stewart Brody was proud of his professional reputation, and did all he could to maintain it. He kept himself fully informed on latest developments in the industry, including the most up-to-date technological aids. He practised the skills needed, maintained his equipment in excellent condition, and kept himself generally fit. He prepared meticulously for each project, and always carried out a post-case assessment, noting ways in which he could further develop his technique. He was not a technician, but a professional. That meant being aware not only of the material context, but the political and social background too. He'd turned down a few projects because he had been unhappy with the possible effects. Talk in the industry suggested that had only enhanced his reputation; people knew he had standards. The personal elimination business was very competitive, and he needed to maintain his position in the industry's premier league, well above the sad psychopaths in the division below him, and the brainless thugs operating in the lesser leagues.

You knew you'd reached the top when you were offered one of those plum jobs that only turn up once in a while. And this was one of them. His target: the UK Chancellor of the Exchequer. Despite the man being well-known, Stewart nevertheless did his homework. It was important to know enough about the target to be able to deal with sudden changes of plan or unexpected interruptions. Usually, he planned the whole project from start to finish: identified the date and location, the method, the appropriate equipment, the exit strategy, and so on. Sometimes, however, the client had specific requirements regarding the project. A frequent request regarding politicians was that the event happen outwith their own country; it was thus possible to blame the killing on international terrorists or political exiles, and then cast aspersions on the local police force for not catching the culprit.

On this occasion it was quite the opposite: the time and place were included in the job specification. It seemed that quite a lot of the planning had already been done by the agency which offered him the project. And it didn't require him to travel too far. No need for a twelve-hour flight, capped by a couple of nights at the Hotel Buongiorno in Djibouti. No, for this one he just needed a couple of nights in Edinburgh. He could have done the job in a day from his home, but for security reasons he always stayed the night before and after a job in a hotel. None of his clients knew where he lived. Except that it was somewhere in Scotland. Perhaps part of the reason for him being given the job was his local knowledge.

The Chancellor was due to make a speech in Edinburgh at a gathering of Tory party donors thinly disguised as a dinner for philanthropists. During the afternoon of that day, however, the great man was being shown some of the businesses of his evening guests. The client had obtained precise details of his itinerary, and had identified what they regarded as the optimum spot for the work. In order to get from the brand-new headquarters of a tax avoidance consultancy to a 'craft defence workshop' manufacturing anti-personnel mines, the minister's convoy would pass along a section of Craigmillar Road, on the city's south side. The short stretch through the housing estate could have been avoided by re-routing the convoy round Edinburgh's crowded ring road, but time was short, as several visits had to be squeezed into a single afternoon. Half way along the stretch was a tall block of flats, Churchill Court, and the specification, sent in coded form to the anonymous email address he used, required the 'elimination consultant' to shoot from a flat on the tenth floor of this block, which would be made available for the occasion.

Stewart didn't like it when other people set the plans. There was no guarantee they'd researched the situation enough, and that was when unexpected contingencies arose. But a contract was a contract, and it specified that the plan supplied would be adhered to. Nevertheless, he visited the block himself a week ahead of the event, to get a good look round. The building, of thirteen storeys, looked down-at-heel. The concrete structure was flaking in parts, but was probably safer that way than if it had been blanketed in garish and highly inflammable plastic cladding. He knew that it had been built in 1966, as a jewel in the council housing crown, but in latter days had acquired a reputation as a haunt of drug-dealers and other criminal elements. Many of the inhabitants had been rehoused, and the bulk of the occupants were now refugees whose applications for residence of asylum were still pending, or elements whose neighbours in other estates had demanded their removal.

As he contemplated the towering structure, Stewart understood why it had been chosen. It did provide a good spot from which to complete the assignment. But it also provided a perfect political context. Political assassinations require a scapegoat; sometimes that's the main point. In this case he guessed the crime would be blamed on a terrorist posing as an asylum-seeker. The siting of the event in Scotland was also politically significant; he suspected Police Scotland and the Scottish Government would be blamed for lax security, and the country itself would be maligned as having since devolution become a haven for foreign criminals and terrorist elements of all kinds.

The day of the event arrived. He'd booked into the Travelodge opposite the Cameron Toll shopping centre the night before. At 2 pm he parked his black VW polo in a side-road off Dalkeith Road. He could have left it in the hotel car park, but leaving it here gave him another option, if he needed to get away quickly. Shouldering his backpack, he walked to Craigmillar Road. He preferred arriving and leaving the scene on foot. Nothing attracted attention so much as a man with a rucksack running out of a building, leaping into a fast car, and roaring off. And there was CCTV there anyway, he'd spotted it on his earlier visit. Luckily it was a sunny day, and the dark glasses and baseball cap were reasonable attire, along with the cheap waterproof jacket and faded jeans. A rather unkempt false hipster beard completed the picture of a plausible resident.

In twenty-three minutes he reached Churchill Court. Pushing the swing door with his foot, he entered the foyer. His first impression was a smell of damp and urine. It reminded him of the supposedly first-class hotel he'd stayed in for an assignment in Tashkent. Using a knuckle, he pressed the button summoning the lift, and selected the tenth floor. The lift was working, although there was a dead mouse lying in one corner. Before getting out, he put on light brown latex gloves.

On the tenth floor, he found the hallway empty, and identified the flat he sought – Flat 10/2. He saw the name on the plastic plate on the door was 'Thatcher'. That made him suspicious. Clearly it was somebody's idea of a joke.

The key to the flat was where he'd been told it would be, under a thick brown doormat, and he knew it wouldn't have been there long. He inserted the key, turned it, and opened the door a little, noting that it seemed quite solid, and peeped into a tiny hallway. It was dark, and a smell of disinfectant wafted out. He took a small torch from his pocket and shone it in, moving it around the small space. Three doors opened off the hallway, all closed. A reflection caught the torch beam. A camera, discreetly positioned in the far corner, on the ceiling. He swung the torchlight onto the edge of the door. There was the Yale lock which he'd used to open the door. But there was another lock a little below it, with no keyhole on either side, and what looked from the size of the socket like a very heavy bolt. Remote-controlled.

He pulled the door shut again, put the key back under the doormat, and took the grey-painted door leading to the staircase. He needed to think. It was clear to him that flat 10/2 was an environment set up and controlled by whoever ran it. There would be cameras throughout so that the occupants could be watched at any time. And the door was designed to ensure the occupant could only enter and leave at the agency's desire. It would no doubt give him an excellent spot from which to fire. But would they let him out afterwards? He didn't like being at somebody else's mercy; that wasn't how he worked.

However, he had a contract, so, as a professional, he would carry out the job. But not from an apartment which could potentially become a prison. He went down to the eighth floor and arrived at Flat 8/2. The name was 'Mbangwo' and someone had spray-painted on the door, 'Blaks fuck of'. He rang the bell. No-one answered. They were probably at some government office filling in a form, or off trying to get the mountain of documents that were demanded as proof of their refugee status. Or maybe at the job centre just trying to get work.

The lock was easily picked, and the flimsy door opened.

There were no extra locks on the door or cameras in the hallway, so he locked the door behind him and went in, passing from the hallway into a bright living-room/kitchen. The furniture in the living room was well-worn, but everything was tidy and clean. Not even a used mug by the sink. A bookshelf contained books about African history and politics. A file lying on the coffee table had the name 'Augustus Mbwango' on the front. He hoped Mr Mbwango would not come back for an hour and would have a good alibi. He touched nothing.

He had about fifteen minutes now. He took off the cap, glasses and beard, then extracted and assembled his rifle, a standard sniper's weapon made in Turkey by a company that also made washing machines and cookers. He opened the doors to the small balcony and knelt on the floor of the living room with the bipod supporting the weapon's muzzle on the balcony. The downward angle was less acute than it would have been from the tenth floor, so he'd get a better shot. The armour-piercing bullets should be enough to deal with the so-called bullet-proof window of the car, as well as the occupant of the rear seat.

Now he waited. An approximate time had been given in his instructions, but exact times could not be guaranteed, and indeed it was ten minutes after the anticipated time that he saw the line of black limousines approaching from the roundabout at the bottom of Dalkeith Road. He checked his position was stable – he had his back against an armchair he'd moved there – and watched through the rifle's telescopic sight.

As they came closer, he focused on the second of the three cars, then on the rear window. Soon he could see the figure behind the glass, recognised the Chancellor's form slumped by the window, no doubt already tired by the endless smiling and back-slapping. He focused in and observed the complacent expression on the lips and the closed eyes. He moved the sights down towards the heart, and his finger tightened on the trigger…

Then it froze. He saw the bloodstain on the white shirt-front. The man was not dozing, he was already dead! Shit. The man had been killed by someone else.

He sat up, thought carefully, as the cars passed on. Why would they want him to shoot a dead man? There was only one answer he could come up with. They wanted to make him the scapegoat. Trap him in the flat and arrest him, then they'd have plenty of evidence he'd done it, and he could be accused of being a home-grown terrorist, a fanatical nationalist. That was why they chose someone based in Scotland. Fake documents would be produced linking him to a fabricated terrorist group. This information would be proclaimed on the BBC as established fact.

He knew the Chancellor had many critics, and enemies within his own party, who saw him as harbouring dangerous ambitions. And his death, whilst removing someone they disliked, would also have the advantage of providing a huge swing towards the party. And give a perfect opportunity for the prime minister to revive her sagging popularity by taking a tough stand against enemies of the state.

He retracted the gun from the balcony, disassembled it, packed his backpack. He had to move fast. They'd no doubt realised he wasn't in the prepared apartment, but would have waited in the hope he'd do the job. Seeing he hadn't, they might think he'd already gone. But he suspected they'd have people in place to arrest him. They didn't know where he was, so he guessed they'd be in or near the building's foyer. He was also sure they didn't know what he looked like. All his correspondence was at a distance from himself, through an online alias. But they'd have an image from the camera in the apartment hallway of a man in a baseball cap with dark glasses and a beard. So they went into his pack, and he took out a yellow hi-visibility waistcoat.

He left the flat and went down the stairs to the third floor. At least Mr Mbwango was in the clear again. In the third floor hall he located the smoke detector, and took out the lighter he always carried, along with the Swiss army knife. In a moment the ear-gagging shriek of fire alarms filled the building. He knocked on all four of the flat doors. A woman in a burka emerged from one.

"Fire brigade," he said. "Come with me and I'll get you out. Have you any children?" She nodded and disappeared.

Meanwhile an old lady had emerged from another flat, who seemed very confused. The other flats must have been empty. When the burka lady returned with three children, he led the group down the stairs, already crowded with people fleeing the alarms. Grenville Court was still a memory too fresh for high-rise dwellers, and nobody was wasting time.

He moved with the human stream into the foyer. It was packed with people, trying to get through the doors, shouting for friends or family. There were even some people trying to go against the tide, up to their flats to get children or parents. Amid the chaos, Stewart recognised two men doing nothing but watch the people passing. He pushed through the crowd towards them. They hadn't seen him yet.

"Hey, you two!" he shouted at them. "What the hell are you doing? This is a bloody emergency! Get these people out of here as fast as you can."

The two men looked at him, processing what he'd shouted. Then one took out an ID card, flashed it. "Special Branch, mate. Get the fuckers out yourself." Then he turned away to watch the stream of people pouring from the stairway.

Stewart gave the men a jovial V-sign, and shepherded the old lady and the family to the door. He led them out into the sunshine, and the crowds waiting on the concrete forecourt. He saw a couple of ambulances parked nearby and led the old lady over. "You'll be able to sit down here," he said to her. A paramedic approached him and he shouted, "Possible smoke inhalation here, can you have a look?" As the man came over, he said to the old lady, "You take care now," waved to the paramedic, and made his way between the two ambulances, shaking off the hi-viz vest, and strolled away.

Back in his room at the hotel, he showered and changed his clothes. Then he put the ones he'd been wearing in a plastic bag, and went to the shopping centre. In the car park was a row of recycling bins, and he tossed the clothes, along with the baseball cap and the beard into the one labelled for fabrics. The dark glasses went into an ordinary waste bin. He went to Waterstones and spotted a reprint of an Edgar Wallace classic, *The Man who was Nobody*. He could read that over his evening meal. Pity about the job, he thought, he would have been well-paid. But he'd find ways of telling the community he'd been set up. That agency would find it hard to get top-class people in future.

Later he watched the news on TV. The BBC merely reported that the Chancellor had had to cancel his speech in Edinburgh through illness. They were clearly still waiting for the official line. STV added that he'd been seen asleep in his car that afternoon, and raised questions about his ability to handle the demands of his job. Stewart remembered the story of the Roman Emperor Numerian who'd been travelling in a closed coach for several hours before someone noticed an unpleasant smell and looked inside, only to find the emperor's decaying corpse.

The Last Ferry

The target emerged, not long after 6.15 pm, from the edifice whose faded splendour recalled a Glasgow whose buildings once proclaimed its prosperity and its pride. At least that was during the day; in the damp winter darkness the upper stories receded discreetly into the gloom, well above the sphere of vision of the wage-slaves scurrying homeward on a cold Thursday night.

He had the photo he'd been supplied with on the screen of his phone, and was able to compare it with the man as he paused in the doorway to light a cigarette. Somewhat under six feet, well-built, fleshy rather than muscular, with a bland face you'd not notice in a crowd, clean-shaven, no glasses, and receding brown hair cut fairly short. He had a green rucksack on his back. There was no doubt, this was target number 53. He knew some people gave them names – Adolf, Vlad, Rasputin, Jack the Ripper, and so on – but he preferred a number. Even a pantomime name could give the target a personality, and once they started becoming human, the job got harder.

Number 53 looked worried. He looked around suspiciously as he sucked on his cigarette. He threw it down half-smoked, and dashed across the road as a gap appeared in the traffic.

Graham followed discreetly as he hurried through the thin drizzle that hung in the street. In five minutes they were in Central Station. His target ignored the giant announcement board looming over the main concourse, and headed for the smaller board at the far end of the station, pausing to study it briefly. He must have a ticket already, probably a season ticket, since he was going home. Graham's instructions told him that was in Rothesay, and he already had his ticket to Wemyss Bay in his pocket.

There was always the chance that number 53 would suddenly decide to do something different. If that were the case, he'd simply do the job tomorrow, and the target would have one more day to live. But number 53 didn't look the sort who'd do something on a whim, and so it proved. In a few minutes he headed for the ticket barrier and on towards platform 15, where plenty of people were already waiting. Five minutes later the train slid alongside the platform. The crowd swarmed to the doors, so that the few people getting off had to push their way through to get away. Graham found a seat where he could keep an eye on number 53, and took a newspaper from his rucksack.

Sure enough, the target stayed on until the terminus, and strode determinedly down the wide passage, floored by wooden beams, that led from the station down to the pier. As Graham walked with the crowd down towards the pier, he noticed the ironwork above and the glistening newly-painted wall panels – he could even smell the paint. He bought a return to Rothesay at the counter in the Calmac waiting room, then joined the queue. The boat had arrived, and the foot passengers were already filing into the ugly grey structure forming an enclosed gangway.

He found himself a seat near the rear of the passenger area on the left side of the boat, close to a door leading out onto a small area of open deck. The rear seating area was divided lengthways by two aisles, so the row he was in only contained four seats. He had the one by the window and put his rucksack on the one next to him. Almost immediately the next seat along was filled by two large plastic bags, and a sharp, musty smell. An old woman dressed in a frayed overcoat and woolly hat sat herself in the end seat.

She offered him a toothless grin. "Gey full, eh? It's aye like this. The last boat, ye ken."

Graham grunted in agreement, scanning the seats visible to him for a sign of the target. Nothing so far. He glanced out the window to see the boat was now moving off.

"Hey, ma friend" – it was the old woman's wheezy voice – "can you move yer baggie, here's my wee nephew come on."

"Sorry," muttered Graham, putting the rucksack down on the floor between his feet. It was immediately replaced by the bulging plastic bags, and the woman moved one seat further in, wafting a miasma of mustiness towards him. He looked up to see the nephew, and there was number 53, sitting down at the end of his row.

"Hi, Auntie Jean, how're you doing?" he said to the old woman, giving her a pat on the arm.

"Ach, aa the better fur seein you." She turned to Graham. "This is ma nephew, Tommy. He's no really ma nephew, we're related somehow, ah kent his parents awfa well. Aye, they looked after me. An Tommy too, he's a good boy right enough. Is that no right, Tommy?"

Number 53 smiled at Graham. "I do ma best for her. Aye, the boat's full today right enough. Maybe something on this evening. Oh, sorry, I'm Tommy McReady." He leaned past the old woman and held out his hand.

"Hi, er, Peter Grace," said Graham.

"You going for a holiday?"

"Just thought I'd have a look at the place."

"Did you no go when you were wee?" put in the old woman.

"I don't remember. But I think this is first time." Avoid getting into a conversation.

The target stood up. "I'm just going for a cuppa tea. I'll get your usual, Auntie? What about you, Peter, can I get you a cuppa? Tea, coffee? Have you tried the mocha, that's what she always has."

"Aye, coffee an chocolate aa mixed up. Real luxury," said Auntie Jean.

"No, I'm OK, really," said Graham. "Thanks." He opened his rucksack, started rummaging about in it. By the time he'd pulled out the novel, number 53 had gone.

"He's a real good lad," said the old woman. "Ah only have mocha on the boat. Ma wee treat. So where is it ye're from, then? Glasgow?"

"No. A bit further away."

"Oh. Edinburgh then?"

"Yes, Edinburgh." That would do. Keep it vague.

"Edinburgh, eh? Aye, well, maybe then you'd no be coming doon the watter for your holidays then. South of France or one o thae posh wee villages in Fife." She grinned. "Only kiddin, son." She looked over towards the central part of the boat where the food and drink counter was situated. "Ach, here comes Tommy now. That was quick."

Graham noticed with a sinking feeling that number 53 was, with great concentration, bringing over a tray with three disposable cups on it. He passed one to the old woman, and then passed the next over towards him. "I thought you might like to try the mocha. Just in case you haven't. You can leave it if you don't want it."

Sometimes trying not to be involved attracts too much attention. Go with the flow. "Thanks, I'll give it a try. Does it need sugar?" He was quite familiar with mocha but didn't want to seem superior.

"Oh, no, I think you'll find it's sweet enough. Just like you, Auntie Jean, eh?"

The old woman cackled loudly. A dog passing down the aisle barked in response.

Graham sipped his mocha and put the cup on the window-ledge. This wasn't a good situation. But he couldn't move somewhere else without attracting attention.

He realised that the target was speaking to him, hurriedly tried to focus. "Sorry, Tommy what was that?" he said. Dammit. He'd used his name. Number 53 had become a person. This was bad.

"I was saying, what is it you do, for work, like?"

"Oh, I'm a consultant. I advise people on, er, business problems."

"I might need to ask your advice. I shouldn't be saying this, Auntie, or burdening you with it, Peter, but I think somebody's after me."

"What do ye mean, Tommy? Surely ye've no got yersel into debt?"

"No, it's worse than that. You see, Peter, I work for a lawyer in town. I'm the messenger and dogsbody. Well, I was sent to deliver a package to an office at the top end of Bath Street. Xynon Resource Facilitation Ltd. An old building, but nicely done up inside. So I'm told to go to the third floor, hand the package in to Room 341. I go up in the lift to the third floor, and the room's right at the end of the corridor. So I hand in the package and get a receipt to take back. That's fine. I'm heading back towards the lift when I trip on my shoelace – it's undone. I'm kneeling down to tie it and I'm just outside this door that's not quite shut. I can hear two guys talking. One of them says, 'I've got it fixed, all right, Simon, but it was tough. I mean, building a block of flats on a toxic waste dump. The planning guy was a bit worried at first, he'd have to lose some of the documentation. I had to offer him another ten grand, but he's OK now. The councillor was trickier, but once I'd shown her a couple of pictures of her on that holiday in Thailand we paid for, she was happy to take the cash and push the application through. Six weeks, we'll be clear.' 'Good work, Ray,' says the other. "We'll make a bomb on that one!'"

"Buildin flats on toxic waste!" said Auntie Jean. "Ah cannae credit ah'm hearin this."

"Well, I'm just getting to my feet when this woman suddenly comes out the door opposite. 'Are you looking for something?' she says, real suspicious like. Of course, this brings one of the guys in the first room to the door, and he sees it's been a wee bit open and I'm outside it. He's a big guy with a nasty look. He drags me into the room, shuts the door, says to me, 'Who the hell are you, pal?' So I tell him who I am and I'm the messenger from the lawyers. 'You hear me,' he says, 'If I think you've been listening to our conversation, I'll have you killed. Now piss off.'

"That was a week ago. I kept quiet all right, and nothing happened, so I thought it was all over. Then I see yesterday's *Daily Chronicle*. Somebody's leaked to the paper that they're going to build on the toxic dump. This morning I get a text message; it just says 'You're dead.' I told the boss my Granny was dying, I'd need a few days off. But I'm sure they're after me now."

"Oh, dearie, what are ye goin to do?" gasped Auntie Jean.

"I'll just go back to the flat, grab some things, and disappear. I can hide up at Davie's place, in Stonehaven. I'll be all right there for a while. What do you think, Peter?"

"It doesn't sound good," said Graham. This was getting worse. Now he found himself empathising with his intended victim. Was it just me they sent, he wondered, or did they put somebody else onto it, just to be on the safe side? "You'd better get away as fast as you can."

"Well," muttered Tommy, "I'd better be on the first boat in the morning, then. Surely they'd not chase me as far as Stonehaven?"

"You'd be better off spending a few weeks in Ireland or

Belgium. But Stonehaven should be OK, as long as you keep your head down, and don't give yourself away. No postcards, letters, emails, phone calls to anybody. Especially not to your family. Don't try to claim benefit or anything. Don't register your existence with anybody. Keep below the radar. Stay indoors for the first month. And change your name."

"That doesn't sound easy. Er, how long would I have to keep it up?"

"I've heard these guys are expensive to hire, and they charge by the day, so after a couple of weeks, it's not cost-effective any more. And if everybody thinks you've been taken out, or you've fled the country, the end result will be the same for them. But to be sure they've forgotten you, I'd give it three or four months. Best plan is, of course, just don't come back at all."

"A new life in Stonehaven?"

"Exactly. And Jean here needs to keep her mouth shut to keep you alive."

"Aye, nae problem. But you're awfy well-informed, Peter. Maybe you're in this business yersel'?" Auntie Jean raised an eyebrow.

She's no daft, thought Graham. "Er, hardly. But in my kind of job, you get to talk to a lot of people. You hear some hair-raising stuff, believe me."

"I'm just popping into the toilet now," said Tommy. "All that tea. Excuse me." He got up and made his way forward, then disappeared through a door on the right.

A couple of minutes later a man sitting four rows in front got up and went into the Gents too. But the way the man moved worried Graham. Almost cat-like, despite his size. And with focus. He needed to be checked out. What was he getting into, thought Graham, now he was getting protective of Tommy? Part of him reflected that if Tommy, no, call him number 53, were killed, that would certainly let him off the hook. But on the other hand…

A minute later the man came out again, a frown on his face. A hard face, stony grey eyes and a nose slightly askew, maybe knocked that way. He walked past Graham's row and through the door behind them. He'd gone on to the after-deck for a smoke, guessed Graham. He needed to check on Tommy right away. The man may just have gone for a pee, but he didn't like the look of him at all.

He went into the toilet. Two urinals, with horizontal bars to hold onto if the ship was rolling, and two cubicles. And no sign of Tommy.

Shit. Now he knew what had happened. The man had come in behind Tommy, probably hit him over the head, dragged him into the cubicle, finished him off there with a knife. Then locked the door from the outside with a short screwdriver. Shit.

He took his own screwdriver from his pocket, turned the bolt, and looked into the cubicle. A fat man with a red face and a bald head was sitting on the toilet, clutching a puzzle book. "Hey, what the hell is this?" he shouted.

"Sorry!" said Graham. "I'm maintenance, I was told one of the doors was jammed shut. Sorry to have disturbed you, sir. Enjoy your stay!" And he shut the door again and relocked it with the screwdriver.

"How many maintenance men do you need on this boat?" continued the bald man's voice. "And don't you talk to each other? What a bunch of cowboys!"

Then other cubicle door swung open and Tommy emerged. "Peter!" he said. "What are you doing here?"

Graham waved him silently out of the door. As soon as they were out, Tommy said, "This is weird. A couple of minutes ago the same thing happened. Some guy opened the next cubicle from the outside, and apologised to the man in it. Said he was maintenance too. What's going on, Peter? Are you involved in this?"

"Don't worry about me, Tommy. But I've heard how these guys operate, and I saw somebody suspicious going into the toilet after you. I think he was a hitman."

"Jeezes! You mean he's on the boat?"

"Yeah. My guess is that when he didn't see you peeing he knew you were in a cubicle. But when he opened the door and met Colonel Mustard there, he realised you weren't alone, and backed out."

"So where do you think he is now?"

"Well, he can't have got off the boat, can he? He'll be lurking somewhere waiting for another opportunity, maybe on the boat, maybe later. Look, Tommy, I know what the man looks like, so I'll take a look round, see if I can spot him. You go back to Aunt Jean as if nothing's happened. Sit in my seat by the window so it's harder for anyone to get at you from the aisle."

He saw Tommy to his seat, then came out onto the deck area at the rear of the passenger lounge. It was windy, and the wind was blowing the rain almost sideways. He saw the man right away, a cigarette in one hand, holding his phone to his ear with the other. Talking insistently to somebody, shouting over the noise of the boat and the wind: "Yeah, yeah, no problems, Mate, job'll be done within the next hour or so, and I'll be back in the morning. And then…" He noticed Graham sauntering toward the rear rail and gave him a malevolent look, then moved away toward the side of the boat, taking up a position leaning on the side rail behind what looked like a square funnel, facing outwards, still talking on the phone.

Graham leaned on the rear rail and looked out onto the dark water behind the ship, seeing the pale gleam of the churned water offering the only evidence of the ship's passage. Beyond that the sea was black and oily, without memory of the moment before.

Then he walked smartly and silently over to the man, knelt swiftly behind him and in one movement gripped his ankles and lifted, pivoting his body on the rail and then flipping him over the side. It was so quick the man didn't even call out. There was just a brief splash, and then the sea forgot him.

Graham looked over the side into the darkness. Only the rush of water pushing past the ship, and the wind in his ear. A dead hitman wouldn't arouse much sympathy, even from his employers. He took from his pocket the cheap pay-as-you-go phone he'd bought that morning, keyed in a number, and sent a text message, "Number 53. Job done. XQ." XQ was his identifier for this job – he never used his own name. He opened the phone, took out the battery and SIM card, put them all in his pocket – they'd go into three different litter bins in Rothesay. He didn't like throwing stuff like that into the sea. A corpse, on the other hand, was soon recycled.

He went back into the lounge, asked Aunt Jean to move her

bags, and sat down between her and Tommy. He whispered to Tommy, "I've had a little chat with the guy. He knows we're onto him. I told him I'd photographed him with my phone, and if he tried anything it would go to the cops. I think he'll keep clear of you now. But we don't want them knowing you're still alive, so the need to vanish still stands." As long as Tommy kept his head down, relocated to Stonehaven, and changed his name, he'd be OK. Sometimes evidence of death was required, but not in this case. Tommy was too small to be that important.

"Wow. Thanks, Peter, you're a real pal. Can I treat you to a meal this evening? There's a couple of great wee restaurants in Rothesay. Or the Victoria's pretty good, you can watch all the folks go past through the big window."

Graham grasped Tommy's thigh with his hand and exerted a lot of force. Tommy's face went white, and he gasped.

"Vanish means vanish, Tommy, if you want to stay alive," he hissed. "Do you understand me?"

Tommy nodded hurriedly.

"Good. Now, I appreciate your offer, but right now you need to go straight home and pack. Don't go out, and don't answer the phone."

"But what about my tea...?"

"Eat whatever's in your fridge. If it's empty, don't eat anything, it'll probably do you good. Now, I'm going to be on the 6.25 boat tomorrow morning back to Wemyss Bay. And if I don't see you on it with a suitcase, I'll find these people and tell them where you are."

"That's right," cackled Jean. "You tell him, son. Sometimes Tommy's a bit slow on the uptake. You're a real pal." And she gave him a big wink.

"Your Calmac ferry has reached its destination," announced an unnaturally jolly voice, "Please prepare to disembark."

Incident on the A81

Elias Kellner knew how to wait. It was his job. He was not a waiter, as the translation from German of his name might suggest, but he knew how to wait. And then, at precisely the right moment, to act. Decisively, discreetly (usually) and fatally. That was his business, and he was one of the best. Elias Kellner was not German; his great-grandfather had moved from a small town on the Baltic coast, not far from Rostock, to the United States. His home was now in another small town, Strutt's Fork, Wisconsin. He had a nice house there, much of it designed by himself, and a nice wife, Lucy-Ann, who was a partner at a local real estate agent. As far as his wife knew, he worked for a company based in Madison who sourced and imported spare parts for farm machinery. As sales manager, he was often obliged to make journeys to Europe, Asia or South America, though these journeys usually only lasted a few days, and it was rare for him to be away for more than a week.

On his latest business trip, in the second week of March, his commission was, as usual, to eliminate a specified individual. The man's name was Bradley Perron. He was a professor at Princeton, an unassuming-looking bespectacled middle-aged man you wouldn't notice even in a crowd of three. But he was doing some ground-breaking work on electrical storage. Leading a revolution in the creation of compact batteries that could store a lot of power, said one article Kellner had read in a popular science magazine. It would make cars running on oil-based fuels obsolete within ten years. Kellner could imagine why some people might want him dead, and was not surprised that his client had approached him. He charged a lot of money, but he was the best.

He waited, in his grey Kia Sportage, in a minor road not far from its junction with the A81, the road which ran from Glasgow north towards Aberfoyle and the Trossachs. He had taken this road from the village of Killearn, heading roughly westward until he parked, half on the overgrown verge, perhaps sixty yards short of the A81. The junction was in fact a crossroads, with the dominant A81 crossed by a minor road running from Killearn to Gartness, and then on by a meandering route towards Drymen. The A81 being the main road, there were STOP signs on both arms of the minor road. This junction was situated half way down a straight stretch of the A81, on which good speeds could be attained, provided a lorry, campervan or farm tractor did not intrude.

Kellner's instructions from his client were that the death of Professor Perron must appear accidental, and that it must occur outwith the USA, preferably on another continent, in order to distance the client, a large oil company, from any suspicion of involvement. His response was to examine the professor's itinerary during a proposed trip to Europe, taking in three major conferences, one in Aberdeen, one in London, and one in Amsterdam. He knew from studies of the professor's previous visits to Europe that he hired a car when in the UK, in order to visit friends and former colleagues from earlier research projects in which British institutions of learning were involved. Kellner's plan therefore was to stage a road accident in which the professor would be fatally injured.

It wouldn't be easy, he knew that. He would have to track the professor's likely routes during his visit and then identify a location where an apparently accidental collision could be engineered. And he had to get hold of a car, sufficiently solid to inflict a good deal of damage, not only on the professor's car, but on the man himself. But he knew where he could obtain such a vehicle, supplied with false registration plates. None of the people he dealt with knew him as Elias Kellner. His documents, which he would destroy on his return to the US, identified him as Henry DuPont, a teacher from Peoria, Illinois, and his story for the inquisitive was that he was in Europe looking for traces of his ancestors in Scotland and in Normandy.

Discovering the professor's itinerary was the easiest bit; the obliging academic had put it on his web page, a sketchy version at first, but with extra details inserted as they were finalised. The version Kellner could see on his phone had been updated just the previous evening, and told him that after spending the night in the village of Bridge of Allan, staying with a senior lecturer at Stirling University who'd worked with him on a research project three years previously, Professor Perron would drive down to Glasgow, where he'd spend the night in a hotel near the airport, before flying on to London early the next morning. The route he would take was, however, not clear: he could take a route running westwards from Stirling, then heading to the Erskine Bridge over the river Clyde, and then south-east for a few miles to the airport, or alternatively he could take the motorway south and then south-westwards into Glasgow and thence to the hotel. But it seemed likely to Kellner that the westward, more rural route would be preferred. The professor had mentioned in blog posts about his foreign trips that he avoided where possible motorways and their European equivalents. He liked to see the real country, rather than its road freight and motor vehicle stock. And he enjoyed being able to relax at the wheel and travel at a speed which would enable him to look around as he went. Kellner guessed this would make him a pain in the ass for other road users, however it would make it easier to track him as he drove.

For this purpose he'd hired the services of another individual, simply named Johnny, recommended by a business associate. Kellner communicated with him using a pay-as-you-go phone, and they never met. Johnny's job was keep track of the professor, confirm that he was sticking to his planned itinerary, and identify the route he would be taking today. Kellner had, on seeing the itinerary, checked out the routes for himself, and identified this particular location as very suitable for his purposes. Johnny had photographed the hire car used by the professor and sent the images to Kellner via WhatsApp. Kellner was pleased to see that it was a light green Vauxhall Astra, easy to keep track of, and not particularly substantial.

He ordered Johnny to watch the house of Dr. Crane, the professor's friend, where that gentleman was staying, and himself waited in a café in Killearn, only a few miles from the chosen junction. He heard nothing until nearly three o'clock. Johnny then reported that he had observed no movement at the house all morning. But at last, at ten to three, the professor had appeared in the front doorway, loaded a suitcase and a smaller case no doubt containing his laptop and its accoutrements into the car, shook hands with his friend, gave the friend's wife a hug, and then got into the car and set off.

Kellner was already aware that the professor was not a fast driver. He therefore instructed Johnny to follow him at a reasonable distance, and to phone him when the green Astra had turned off the road running from Stirling to Dumbarton onto the A81 running south. There was a small chance the professor might stay on the Dumbarton road in order to see the bottom end of Loch Lomond at Balloch, in which case Kellner would have to get himself very quickly to an alternative location near a garden centre on the road into Balloch. However, the lateness of the professor's departure encouraged Kellner to think the route by which he was waiting was the most likely. It was also the one which would be recommended by the SatNav in the professor's car. Fortunately, a third possible route had been ruled out since a bridge at the village of Croftamie had partially collapsed the previous year due to subsidence caused by the fast-flowing burn it crossed, and had not yet been repaired.

Kellner left the café and returned to his car. He was satisfied to note that the weather was good for the operation: cool and cloudy, but not raining. He read online that this was typical for Scotland in August. He would be able to spot the green Astra without difficulty. At quarter to four he drove out of the village on the Gartness Road and parked half on the verge a few yards short of the junction.

At five to four the call came from Johnny: the car had indeed turned onto the A81. And the professor's average speed since leaving the house was 45 mph. He would arrive at the junction in about seven minutes.

After five minutes, Kellner moved the car off the verge and stationed it at the cross-roads, directly by the STOP sign. He could see up the road on his right as far as a bend about three hundred yards away. Now he just had to wait. Of course, there was always a chance that some other vehicle would come along the road he was parked in and wonder why he wasn't moving. But that didn't happen.

He spotted the green Astra as soon as it rounded the bend. There was no other traffic on the road. Whilst a multi-vehicle pile-up could easily prove fatal to the professor, there was no guarantee, and with several vehicles involved, lots of people would be on the scene fairly quickly. That was not what he wanted, for if the crash did not prove fatal to the driver of the green Astra, Kellner was ready to turn up at the scene as a witness, and discreetly administer a dose of Potassium Chloride. Fifty milligrammes would be enough to trigger what would look just like a heart attack. And very plausible too, as the outcome, for a man getting on in years, of a traumatic car crash.

As the car approached he eased forward, ready to stab the accelerator pedal at the right moment.

3…2…1…now!

The car kicked forward, smashing into the Astra as it passed, just behind the rear door. As he'd hoped, the Astra's rear end skidded across the road, dragging the rest of vehicle round. This is where a 30-ton truck coming the other way would have been useful, but sadly, the road remained clear. The Astra slewed across the road, still moving forward, mounted the opposite verge and its driver's side whacked into a tree.

Nice, thought Kellner. But he'd still need to check the professor was dead and finish him off if that wasn't the case. So he drove across the road into the entrance of the Gartness Road, parked by the roadside, and got out. The high bank at the edge of the road, and the vegetation on top of it, screened him from view from the A81. He first inspected his car for damage at the front. The number plate was gone, and there were some dents and scratches on the bonnet, but no substantial crumpling or rupturing; the car had been well-chosen for him, and he'd asked for some extra strengthening inside the bonnet. The discreet repair workshop and vehicle supplier in Dumbarton, privately recommended to him, had done well. He checked the hypodermic was in his inside pocket, and walked back to the main road to get to the crashed Astra.

The first thing he noticed as he came round the corner, and the crash site became visible, was the people. Two men and two women, in their twenties or thirties by the look of it. Their car, a red people carrier, was parked beyond the crashed Astra. The two women were at the driver's side of the crashed vehicle, peering in the window. One of the men was photographing the damage on the Astra with his phone, while the other one was talking on his phone, perhaps summoning an ambulance or the police. He would have to be careful.

He slipped his dark glasses on, and assumed a concerned expression before proceeding on towards the scene. He approached the man photographing, waved a greeting, and asked what had happened. He used a polite English accent. The lessons he'd taken from the speech coach several years ago continued to come in useful.

"There's been a bump," said the man. "Some idiot came out of the side road and ran into this guy's car. He's lucky. If we'd been coming up the road a few seconds earlier, he'd have gone right into us and that would have been a very nasty smash. As it is there's an impressive bash on both sides of his car, but I don't reckon he's badly hurt."

"Anything I can do to help? I have some medical experience," said Kellner. There was still a chance he could finish the target off if he could get near him and on his own. "Perhaps I could have a look at him?"

"You'd better ask Sharon and Janette. But they're both nurses, so I think they've got it covered. By the way, did you happen to see anything? Which way were you travelling?"

"Oh. I was about to pull out from the Gartness road when I noticed the two cars here. So I backed off the road again and came here to see if there was anything I could do. Do you happen to know who did this? I mean, what sort of vehicle?"

"Yes, I saw it cross the road and go into the road where I guess you're parked. Big grey one. Not a Range Rover, but something in that range."

"Sportage!" came a shout from the other man.

"What was that, Dave?"

The second man came up. "Might have been a Kia Sportage. Andy at the gym has one, and that car looked quite like it."

The first man addressed Kellner again. "If you're down that road, it must have passed you."

"I didn't encounter any big grey car," he answered, "but he could easily have pulled into a farm lane when he saw me coming. I don't drive very fast."

"OK, thanks. The guy's car's still driveable. Just! So I'll suggest we get his car and ours off this main road – I don't want anyone rushing round that corner and smacking into us. Is there room where you're parked?"

"Yes," said Kellner. "Tell you what, I'll nip back and move my car so there's enough room for your car and his. I'll be back in a sec."

He turned and started walking back without waiting for a response. He'd concluded it was time to clear off now. With two nurses on the scene, he wouldn't have much chance to get at the professor unobserved. And as soon as the two men saw his car, a Kia Sportage, with recent damage to the bonnet, they'd put two and two together. They didn't look stupid. And the one who was phoning had finished; that told him it wouldn't be long before they started hearing the sirens.

His original plan had been, after disposing of the professor, to make off up the A81 and then turn left a couple of miles up to make for Balloch and then Dumbarton, where the anonymous vehicle workshop would receive his car and make it disappear. He'd checked out the Gartness road as a Plan B one evening; after the village the road shrank to single track, wide enough only for a single vehicle. However, he'd encountered very little traffic, and the road, after much wending about, came out onto the Stirling-Dumbarton road near Drymen, which was the right direction for him. It would do as a backup plan.

As soon as he got to the car, he knew it was going to be Plan B. If the man who'd reported the incident had identified the colour and type of car, and police were already on the way, the missing number plate would be enough to arouse suspicion. He drove off rapidly towards Gartness.

He passed through the village with no problems, and then entered the single track portion of the road. He made good progress for about three miles, encountering no other traffic apart from two cyclists who'd wisely pulled into a passing place to let him through. Then his luck ran out. He rounded a tight bend to see a very large tractor filling the road ahead. Worse still, he then saw that it was towing a trailer piled high with hay bales. He threw on the brakes and skidded to a halt nose to nose with the tractor. He hit the horn and waved the tractor to reverse and find a passing place or a farm track to get into. After all, the driver, being a local farmer, would know the road far better than he.

The farmer looked down on him with a slight smile and shook his head. For a minute neither moved. Then the tractor driver opened his door and began to climb down. This wasn't good. The last thing Kellner wanted was a conversation which the driver would later remember. He could of course simply kill him, but his vehicle would still be blocking the road, and extra killings in the course of an assignment were an unpredictable risk. His best course now was to retrace his route and hope he could get across the A81 and onto the Killearn road without being intercepted.

As the tractor driver strolled towards him, he reversed the car rapidly to his left onto the verge until the rear hit and then pushed over a fence, then spun the steering wheel to the right and accelerated. The left edge of the bonnet scraped along the old stone wall bordering the road, but he got round, and put his foot down to head back to the crossroads.

He soon came up behind the two cyclists, who were struggling up a hill and paid no attention to his horn. His only option was to come up slowly to each one, and simply nudge them off the road into the ditch which now ran alongside. That done, he continued on without further incident to the village and passed through again.

Soon he was almost at the crossroads again. As he came round a bend he saw the spot he'd parked at earlier. But now it was crowded. There was the crumpled Astra, the professor himself standing beside it talking to a police officer. The police car and the red people carrier were there too, and beyond them, its rear almost flush with the main A81, was an ambulance. Between the am-bulance and the police car, a group of people could be seen talking.

As soon as he saw them, they saw him too. The professor and the police officer both glanced at his car. Then the professor pointed and shouted something. He wasn't going to able to sneak past. The policeman stepped forward and raised his hand. Time for action.

He rammed his foot down and sped towards them, his hand on the horn. The officer leapt out of the way as he shot past. He glimpsed the open-mouthed expressions of the group by the ambulance. Then he was at the crossroads. He stabbed on the brake, and glanced to his left. The road was clear and he pulled out to head north.

Into the path of a truck loaded with thirty tons of felled timber. And moving at fifty miles an hour, that's a lot of kinetic energy, and it's going to pack a hell of a punch.

After the initial impact, Kellner lived for perhaps another two or three seconds. That impact crushed his car to perhaps half its usual width. Then the front wheels of the lorry mounted the wreckage and the whole vehicle and its cargo crunched over the flattened remains before the driver could bring it to a halt a hundred yards further on.

The fatal accident inquiry held the following week determined that Henry DuPont, an American who would be used to driving on the left, had, in the absence of other traffic, and in a hurry to escape from the scene of a previous collision which he seemed to have caused, had momentarily forgotten that he was in the UK, and simply looked the wrong way before pulling out. The lorry driver was fully exonerated; he had done all he could to bring his vehicle to a stop. A couple of days later Police Scotland were informed by their colleagues in Illinois that no trace could be found of any Henry Dupont who could be linked with the papers of the dead man. The DNA and fingerprints of the dead man drew no match on the police databases in the US. The Peoria Police Department suggested the papers might be false.

By this time Lucy-Ann Kellner, of Strutt's Fork, Wisconsin, had approached the authorities to report her husband Elias Kellner missing. Inquiries with his employers showed that no person of his name or description worked for them. No attempt was made to obtain a sample of Mr Kellner's DNA from items which could be provided by Mrs Kellner. The local police, being informed of his frequent absences, concluded that he was involved in some sort of criminal operation, possibly drug trafficking, and that, for reasons connected to this, he had simply abandoned his life in Strutt's Fork, to continue his criminal career, under another name, in some other part of the country. After questioning her at length about her husband's life and activities, they concluded she was an innocent dupe, and advised her to forget him and move on.

A Meeting in Berlin
Part I

The terminal at Tempelhof Airport in Berlin is the largest extant building from the Fascist era in Europe. It was designed in the shape, seen from above, of an eagle in flight. But the huge building, incorporating aircraft hangars as well as passenger and freight terminal facilities, was still uncompleted by 1939 and was used during the war as an aircraft assembly plant. After the war, Tempelhof became West Berlin's airport, famously used during the Berlin Airlift from June 1948 until September 1949, and finally closed in 2008. The runway areas are used as a recreation space for Berliners, and the city authorities are keen to find uses for the many chambers of the terminal building.

Thus, half way along a bland and dimly-lit corridor was found a door, behind which lay an office, a meeting room, a small kitchen and a toilet. The only windows were at the far end of the meeting room, which looked over the wide green space where citizens walked, jogged, played football, and passed the time of day. On the door, as on every other door on the corridor, was a blue plastic plate about the size of a postcard, on which was etched in white the name of the company or organisation whose space lay behind the door. In this case, the plate read simply, 'The Cerialis Foundation,' with, below, in German, 'Cerialis Stiftung.'

But the name did not refer to the Roman cognomen Cerialis, meaning 'of Ceres,' nor to its most celebrated holder Quintus Petillius Cerialis Caesius Rufus, successful general and one-time governor of the province of Britannia. It was simply a play on words, for behind the off-white walls of the corridor and the grey door with the blue plaque lay the headquarters of the League of Ethical Assassins.

The League, as we shall call it from now on, has a long history, being founded not long after the failed revolutions of 1848 by a small group of people who felt that extremes of evil should be met by equally extreme solutions. They spent the next twenty years harmlessly debating the nature of evil, until, in 1868, an unknown assassin killed an arms manufacturer who had made a huge fortune supplying both sides in the American Civil War; the businessman had even boasted of it as evidence of the value of capitalism as a stimulant of world progress. The assassin applied to join the League, and the period of philosophising was over. Actions replaced words. Much discussion preceded each action, and much preparation followed each decision, so that the deaths of industrialists, politicians, generals and others were never solved. In many cases they were put down to accidents or natural causes. The League was never sure if its actions made any difference to the world. They realised that capitalism, autocracy, elitism and cruelty could not be erased overnight, or changed by the erasure of particular individuals, but believed that, on balance, if one had the capacity to make some small change, one should make the effort.

Occasionally, word got out about the League's activities. The author Edgar Wallace caught a whisper and promised to say nothing. But financial pressures led him to publish his successful novel *The Four Just Men*, presenting a rather simplified version of the League. Despite being warned by the League not to do it, Wallace published not one but two sequels. Finally, in 1933, while in the US working on the script of the epic monster movie King Kong, he collapsed and died. The doctors concluded he had suffered from undiagnosed diabetes. And that is what the world thought.

The League's activities were not always successful. Two attempts to assassinate Adolf Hitler failed, though the would-be assassins were not caught. After that it was judged too dangerous, for the League's rules did not permit suicide attacks, or activities, such as bombings, which could result in terrorising whole populations. There was also the issue of retaliation. The attempts on Hitler had been followed by widespread persecution of innocent groups who were blamed for the outrages.

So the League continued its work, quietly and efficiently taking out American gangsters, Italian Mafiosi, and dangerous politicians among others. Perhaps its greatest achievement was the death of Joseph Stalin. Even though it did not end the Soviet regime's authoritarianism and imperialism, the dictator's death did lead to an end to his excesses, and in the years following many lived who would otherwise have died.

Now, in the twenty-first century, the League still had work to do. And new challenges to meet.

Six persons, four men and two women, sat round the conference table in the meeting room, one at the head of the table, one at the foot, and the four others on one side, so that all could see, and be seen by, the six figures appearing on the monitor screens ranged along the table against the side wall. This was not the full membership of the League; there were four apologies, and it was not expected that the three emeritus members, now well into their seventies, should attend, though their views on the main issue had been canvassed by email. All the attendees, including the virtual ones, were masked. Covid, in fact, had made no difference to this essential aspect of the League's procedures. The other important aspect that all observed was the use of pseudonyms. Fundamental to the League's safe operating was the principle that no member should know the personal details of another. So there would be no friendly gathering in a cafe or restaurant after the meeting, no birthday greetings or congratulations on some new personal achievement. That was the way it had to be.

The meeting was to commence at 11 am, Central European Time. For convenience of the multinational group, the language used was English. For two of those present it was their mother tongue; for the rest their second or third language. The chair had been chosen at random from those members who had indicated their willingness to attend in person, for there was no hierarchy in the League. She was a tall, slim woman, her black hair straight with a fringe, like Cleopatra. Appropriate, though her slight accent did not betray her Greek origin. None of those present knew that she was in reality Theodora Passolis, a top executive in a small pharmaceutical company based in the city of Preveza, in the north-west of the country. Her image did not appear on the company's website, which was only available in Greek, and did not attract many visitors. Her poisons had ended the lives of eighteen persons whom the group had considered a threat to democracy or to peace in different parts of the world.

"Welcome to the meeting, ladies and gentlemen," she said. "We have one topic on the agenda, the question of serial killers in literature. As you are aware, most of us could be classed as serial killers, in that we have killed more than once, and may well do so again. However, our eliminations are ethical, based on the shared belief that evil members of society are best removed from it altogether, and every mission we mount requires the approval of at least two-thirds of us at a meeting. There are, as we know, a very small number of individuals also identified as serial killers. These are criminals, whose desire to kill arises out of various psychological issues. These are evil individuals, overwhelming male, rightly incarcerated as soon as they are apprehended. You will all know some of their names: Luis Garavito, Javed Iqbal, Mikhail Popkov, Wang Qiang, Ted Bundy, and so on. They are found in every continent, probably in every age. But the fact remains that they are very few and far between. It is only their notoriety which gives the impression that they are many. They are not the reason for this meeting.

"There has, over the past thirty years, however, grown up a vast literature of fictional serial killers. They occur much more frequently in crime fiction that they do in reality. And as time has passed, they are portrayed as crazier and crazier. For a crime novel to win a prize now, the serial killer must be completely insane, but appear perfectly normal. Yet when he, and they usually are male, seizes his victim, he must perform the most disgusting and absurd mutilations of her body, and, by the way, it usually is a she. Branding symbols, carving biblical quotations, placing the victim in a special pose to represent a nursery rhyme or an old master painting, removing some or all of the internal organs, scalping, skinning, decapitating, and so on. And our problem is that this has affected the public perception of serial killers. People now think that most murderers are in fact serial killers, although statistics show this is completely the opposite of the truth. And ethical assassins like ourselves are branded as lunatics. These writers are, in a word, giving us a bad name. And we have therefore received a proposal that we take action."

"The proposal, submitted by Mr Schmidt, is that we take

action against some of the more prolific and popular authors within this genre."

One of those on the screens raised a hand.

"Mr Kowalski, please."

The man known to them as Kowalski, leaned forward. His real name was Jesus Disarronno; he had brought about the sudden deaths of six top Mafiosi through apparent accidents: a gate failure at a level crossing, a collapsing balcony on a new building, a trip on a staircase, a fall from a mountain path, all completely plausible. "I can see the problem. But these are not evil people. They are perhaps thoughtless, but not evil. I don't see it as our role to kill people who are merely thoughtless. We should identify exactly where the evil is here. Is it the authors, or the readers, the agents or the publishers? Or the newspapers and magazines who promote real serial killers as if they were celebrities, and rave about the serial killer fiction in their so-called culture pages? Don't get me wrong. I agree that some action is necessary. I am raising the question of exactly what action is appropriate. And is in line with the objectives of our group."

These words were met with nods and murmurs of approval both around the table and on the screens. Two of the screens showed a thumbs up animation in the top left hand corner.

"Thank you, Mr Kowalski," said the chair, "there is clearly some support for your proposal. Do we have someone who can throw some more light on the situation?"

The other woman in the room raised her hand. Her real name was Ilona Vortsova. She lived in a small house on the edge of Yakutsk, and was an air stewardess with SiberiAir. She was also an amateur actress with a small theatre company, The People's Players of Yakutia. She had, through almost invisible micro-injections administered in Business Class, brought about the death by fatal heart attack of four billionaire oligarchs, each of whom had become rich by stealing what had been built up and paid for through the taxes of millions of ordinary Russian citizens. How many had died because money was diverted from hospitals, public transport, food and shelter, to the pockets of these men was incalculable.

"Ms Smith, please," said the chair.

"Mr Kowalski is correct. This is not a sickness of the authors, it belongs to the system which sponsors the desire among people to read such material. I would say the blame must be divided. The authors are not innocent, for they create these works knowing they feed a market that will make them rich. I should add that few of these authors actually are rich. The profits go to the agents and publishers, and to the multinational corporations which own the publishers. But again, none of these are innocent. They knowingly manipulate people's desires, for gain, without caring how what they do affects people's understanding of the world. They are, between them, creating what is in effect fake news, a perception that something which is rare is in fact common. This distracts attention from the real problem, which is the casual violence of men towards women."

"Do you have a proposal for us, Ms Smith?"

Part II

Gwendoline Foster-Tanqueray was a best-selling author of crime fiction. Her novels, eleven so far, featured the Serial Killer Unit of London's Metropolitan Police, headed by Chief Inspector Juliette Manchego, who led a team of suitably diverse and inclusive individuals. A significant part of the team was psychologist Sulieman Djugashvili, whose insights into the crazed minds of her killers brought to light the most bizarre and outrageous re-imaginings of the nature of reality. 'Reality is not as we know it,' was his favourite phrase, and other more Delphic utterances peppered his lectures to the gathered team.

One Monday Gwendoline, who lived in a little village on the Sussex Downs, received an email from her agent, Samantha Carplethwaite. 'Darling,' it read, 'Do come in on Wednesday. Ten thirty OK? Big deal in offing with US publishers. SCB xxxx.' Gwendoline was very excited. This could be a big breakthrough. The US market was huge, and the appetite for serial killers possibly even greater than in Britain. All through Monday and Tuesday she grew more excited, even forgetting to feed her cat on Tuesday. Dear Fluffy brought her a dead starling to remind her, and she was most apologetic as she spooned the top-class gunge out of the tin.

She was up at six thirty on Wednesday, for a shower and hair wash, had her usual cup of rose hip and kale tea for breakfast, and headed out. It was a fine summer morning. The birds were singing, and everything was good. She drove to Pinglewold Station, and caught the 8.15 to Victoria. Then she headed for the underground. It was just after 9.30, but the corridors and platforms were hoaching with people. The smell of sweat and aftershave and perfume and last night's wine and cigarettes swam around in the foetid passages like a host of insects. She made it to the platform. Soon she would hold the contract in her hand, and would then be starring in those huge crime festivals they had over there. This crush and stink was worth it.

She never saw who gave her that little nudge, just as the train pulled in, never felt anything beyond the first blinding crunching screeching explosion as the train wheel crushed her spine, ribs and then her skull, all within two seconds, maybe even one.

Meanwhile Samantha was heading for the little cafe in Soho to which Gwendoline had invited her. 'Meet you there at eleven,' the email had said. 'Got some great news. You won't believe it. :-) xx' Samantha naturally wondered what the great news could be. Probably she'd just managed to finish the tenth book. That would be good news, as Samantha felt Gwendoline was running out of ideas. The last three had been very similar, and more about the love-lives of the team than the serial killer and his obsession. Julian, at the publishers, had been suggesting they might not take the next one, unless it focused more on the killer and his mutilation of the women he chose for his victims.

She reached the cafe early, sat at one of the outside tables, and ordered an Americano with soya milk on the side. It was a hot day, but the cafe had canopies over the tables, and she was thankful she wasn't inside. This wasn't a bad choice, she had to admit, she hadn't thought Gwendoline was that savvy when it came to cafes. She was just about to take a sip of coffee, when she heard a cry.

"Sam, is that you, darling? How amazing. I didn't realise you frequented Geppetto's."

The owner of the voice was a slim woman in sandals, a short summer dress, a big hat and sunglasses. Samantha had no idea who she was. Probably one of those wannabe authors who pestered her at book festivals, pretending to be friends of one of the well-known authors on her list. On the other hand, it might be someone it was useful to know.

"Hi," she replied. "I come here now and again. I'm just waiting for someone now."

"That's all right, Sam darling, I'll be out of your way in a minute." The woman sat down, with a cheesy grin. "I'm on my way to collect some ARCs."

ARCs. Advance Reader Copies. So this could be someone in the publishing business.

"Oh, which book?" she asked. This would give her a clue as to who this was.

The woman was about to answer when something seemed to catch her eye. She clutched Samantha's arm. "Oh my God! Look over there. Isn't that Val Renahan? You know, the Booker longlist. Wow, he's a hunk!"

Samantha looked over to where she was pointing. Who the hell was she pointing at? There was a tall man with a panama hat and a beard, but that wasn't him. Was it?

The woman got up suddenly. "Sorry, Sam dear, I really must have a word with Val. See you soon." She moved off and rushed across the road, dodging the traffic, and disappeared into the crowd. Samantha breathed a sigh of relief and took a long slug of coffee. The plastic tablecloth clipped to the table top, with scenes from Disney's Pinocchio was the last thing she ever saw. Across the road, the woman in the hat watched carefully, to be sure Samantha had dropped the mug and the contents had drained away.

Julian Phillipps-Windsor glanced at his Rolex. Nearly twelve. He'd better go. Samantha Carple-Thingy wanted to see him. About Gwendoline Whatsit's next book. Her email claimed it was a cracker, the best she'd written, great literary quality worth a shot at a prize. Yeah, right. Julian didn't care a damn about literary quality, most of that stuff was just pretension anyway. His job was taking on books that would sell, and that meant Gwendy would have to put a lot more gore into her next opus. They'd been offered another book by a debut author, in which the killer turns his victims into giant marionettes, and gives performances at obscure literary festivals. That might be a goer.

He got up. At least he didn't have to go far; Samantha had suggested meeting at one of the benches in the piazza just outside the glass wedge that was the head office of Blood-Red Books Ltd.

He didn't see her, but then, he was a few minutes early. He sat down on the first empty bench he came to. Even in his shirt-sleeves he could feel the heat. He should have put his hat on to come out. Still, he could only afford to give her ten minutes of his time. Time was money after all. And he had an appointment with Jason Meakin on the top floor at half past. The top man on the top floor. Did this mean promotion? Jason's email suggested it was good news.

He glanced at a woman along the piazza in the direction of the office. Sandals, short summer dress, nice legs, good figure in fact, blond hair, dark glasses, floppy hat. He could imagine her in a film. As she walked past, she halted, appeared puzzled, then turned to him.

"*Excusez-moi*," she said with a smile, "*Je cherche*, oh, I'm sorry, I seek the office of the Blood-Red Books. I think it's here, but I do not see it. Can you help me?"

"Of course, Mademoiselle," he said, jumping to his feet. "It's just over there. But I can take you there myself, I work there."

"But that is merveilleux," she simpered, and began to walk alongside him. "There is a person I must see there. I have his name here." She dug her hand into the handbag which hung on her shoulder.

He could smell her perfume, imagine the contours of her body, the feel of her skin. "I'll take you there myself. Maybe we could have coffee afterwards. There's a lovely little cafe the other side of the piazza." He moved closer to her, waiting for the business card which she would pull out of the handbag.

The card came out, but she stumbled on something and

dropped it. As they both knelt to pick it up, they bumped into each other, and he didn't notice the tiny pinprick in his thigh.

"Ah! *Excusez-moi!*" she said. Those were the last words he ever heard.

Jason Meakin was interrupted. He had the windows of his top-floor office open, and there seemed to be some commotion in the street below. Julian Phillipps-Windsor had emailed asking to see him at twelve fifteen, said it was urgent. The idiot was already late. He got up and moved to the window, looked down into the piazza to see what the noise was. A small crowd had gathered, not far from the entrance to the building. Curious, he opened the French window and stepped out onto the narrow balcony which graced the top floor offices. It was very useful for confidential meetings, with just enough room for two chairs and a small table, just right for a couple of coffees or G & Ts. He was just leaning over the balcony railing thinking of a cool gin and tonic and trying to see what was going on down below when the dart, fired from the roof of another building nearly half a mile away, hit him in the chest.

"What the fuck?" he gasped, pulling it out and staring at it. Then everything began to sway and he wobbled right over the railing.

The following day two articles appeared in two different newspapers. In the popular *Daily Bugle*, a report headed 'Serial Killer Genre is Cursed' quoted a 'renowned Bulgarian medium' as saying that there was a mysterious supernatural connection between the coincidental deaths of Gwendoline Foster-Tanqueray, who had accidentally fallen to her death at a crowded tube station, her agent Samantha Carplethwaite, who had collapsed and died of what appeared to be heatstroke at a Soho cafe, her publisher, Julian Phillipps-Windsor, who had died outside his office of a heart attack, and Blood-Red Books boss Jason Meakin, who had accidentally fallen from the balcony outside his sixth-floor office. The medium, known only as Madame Blagovitsa, asserted that the serial killer genre was cursed because, 'these writers have tampered with dark forces, and the forces of darkness have struck back.' She warned that others connected with the genre would die unless they moved away to some other subject. She suggested historical romances as the way forward: 'for these books are blessed by the forces of light.'

Meanwhile, in the more up-market *London Intelligencer*, in its influential culture pages, literary critic Edward Pope-Lannister had a piece entitled, 'The End of a Genre.' He suggested that the serial killer genre had now run its course, having become boring and repetitive, and most of all, out of touch with reality. Crime fiction readers, he claimed, were now seeking more 'whimsical and aspirational' forms of crime fiction, in line with the spirit of the more confident and prosperous times that were coming with Brexit and the end of Covid. He urged publishers and bookshops to divest themselves of this 'washed-out genre of fantastically absurd lunatic mass-murderers' and pay more attention to what customers really wanted.

That afternoon, in an office in Berlin, a masked woman studied the two reports on the screen of her laptop. Standing behind her, another woman, also masked, looked down over her shoulder at the screen.

"The plan was a good one, Ms Smith," said the sitting woman.

"Yes," replied the other, "it turned out well. Now perhaps our work will not be dismissed as that of lunatics."

"You are right," said the sitting woman. "The world still needs us. You were mentioning earlier the Prime Minister of England, I believe..."

A Man's Drink

Detective Inspector Dyer was on his second cup of coffee and page 7 of Monday's *Courier* when Sergeant Craib put his head round the door.

"Fatal incident, inspector," reported the man in uniform. "House between Crieff and Comrie. A man's been shot. May need your attention."

"Details?"

"A 999 call came in at 09.22. Nearest patrol car attended scene. Officers Stonier and Williamson. 09.40 they called me. Site secured. SOCOs are on the way."

Dyer threw down his paper. "Thank you, sergeant. I'm onto it. I'll take Langford."

"Ah, well, sir, there's a wee problem there. Sergeant Langford phoned in on Saturday morning to say he'd tested positive. Out with the lads Friday evening, so I contacted the others. Wilson was positive too, Scotson and Cunningham are self-isolating."

Dyer scowled. Now he'd have to take one of the women. "What about Armstrong?"

"Sorry, sir, she's on leave till Wednesday. Down in the Borders walking. Her phone's off. But you're in luck. Clements is in."

Dyer cursed inwardly. Detective Constable Ann Clements was the last person he wanted to work with. Transferred a year ago from Paisley after she complained about sexual harassment by fellow officers. None of the men like a clype, so they kept their distance. As a single mother, with two children to look after, she also avoided the social events. Not a team player, concluded Dyer.

"You. With me," was all Dyer said to her. He was silent in the car as he drove to the incident location. She didn't ask about it. Presumably Craib had told her.

"What a place!" she said as they turned into the drive. A tasteful blend of timber, stone and glass, perched on a rocky knoll, the steep slope of the hill behind it. A broad balcony of decking protruded beyond the rock, supported by angled wooden beams.

Dyer did not respond.

At the rear of the house, they exited the car. Dyer tall and slim, with what used to be called a military bearing, Clements, shorter and bulkier, still carrying the extra weight she'd put on after giving birth six years previously.

PC Williamson stood at the main door of the house. "In here, sir, then left, and at the end," he said as they approached. Dyer ignored him and went in. Clements said hello. Williamson looked at his feet.

They entered a hallway, bright with daylight from above. To the right and left, doorways. Then on the right a staircase, and finally, ahead of them, a corridor, running left and right.

They turned left into the corridor. The first doorway on the right opened into a living-room. French windows offered a spectacular view across the green floor of Strathearn to the hills at its southern edge. A woman sitting in an armchair got up as they looked in.

"Deal with her," ordered Dyer, and moved on to the next doorway.

The dead man sat upright at his desk, his head against the padded upholstery of his top of the range office chair, his arms resting on his desk. By his right hand was a glass of whisky. The bottle, two-thirds full, stood nearby. Facing him across the desk was an upright chair with upholstered back and arms. There was little else in the room. Except for the glass-fronted cabinets filling the wall facing the dead man, on whose shelves rested row after row of whisky bottles.

Two forensics officers in white suits, known by all as Thing One and Thing Two, moved quietly about the room.

"What have you got?" demanded Dyer.

"Dead man," said Thing One, evidently male, "shot in the left eye. Bullet passed through rear of the skull, lodged in the headrest of his chair."

"Trajectory?"

"Slightly upwards. Shooter probably sitting in the chair

opposite. Or kneeling behind it. Or a dwarf. You want a look? Take ten minutes, we could do with a cuppa. You'll need a suit. I'll get a couple."

"One's enough."

Five minutes later Dyer entered the room, treading carefully in the white one-piece suit, and flexing his gloved fingers. Clements stood in the doorway.

"Who is he?" snapped Dyer.

"Steven McIlmer. CEO of Worldwide Whisky Tours. Trips to distilleries all over the globe. Tastings and workshops included, accommodation in luxury hotels. Personally led by Mr. McIlmer. Author of six books about whisky."

"Who's the woman through there?"

"His PA. Janet Stanton. She found the body, about 9.20 this morning. Called 999."

"Ask her if he had an appointment last night?"

"I did. He didn't."

"Well, seems obvious what happened. Someone came in, probably a burglar, found McIlmer here drinking whisky. Sat in the chair facing him. Shot him. Then panicked and fled. Probably no money lying around."

"Round up the usual suspects?" suggested Clements.

Dyer stared at her. "Try to be funny with me again, young lady, and I'll have you back in uniform and transferred back to Paisley. Got that?"

"Yes, sir. Sorry, sir. Er, that's an unusual glass, isn't it?"

"It's a whisky tasting glass. Heavy base, wider bit where you can swirl the spirit around, narrower part at the top, captures the scent."

"Is it whisky he's drinking?"

"Obviously." Dyer picked up the glass in his gloved hand, peered at the golden liquid, swirled it around, and gently sniffed. "Nice. Heavy but not smoky. A hint of seaweed." He drew in another breath and let it fill his lungs. "Islay, I'd say."

"You certainly know your whisky, sir," said Clements.

"It's a man's drink, is whisky."

Clements pointed to the bottle. "But what's in there's a slightly different colour."

Dyer frowned at the bottle, then picked it up and looked at the label. "That's odd." He swirled the liquid in it, pulled out the cork and breathed the vapour. "This is not what's in the glass. This is lighter. As even you noticed, the colour's paler." He inhaled again. "The scent is gorse, and heather. This is a Dalpittrie, from Speyside. Other side of the country from Islay."

"So the whisky in the glass didn't come from that bottle?"

Dyer ignored the question. "It's a puzzle," he muttered to himself. Dyer didn't like puzzles.

"Sir, er, perhaps the killer swapped the bottles. After he'd shot McIlmer. He could hold McIlmer's hand round the new bottle to leave his prints there."

"That's absurd. Why would he do that?"

"Maybe he didn't want the first bottle to be seen. So he picked one off the shelves, and put the first bottle in its place. But all those bottles. It could be anywhere."

Dyer turned to the cabinets and stared, running his eyes over the labels. "They're not in alphabetical order."

"Why don't we ask Ms Stanton?"

"Get her."

A moment later Janet Stanton stood in the doorway, a slim figure, her long black hair in a loose ponytail. "How can I help?" she asked politely.

"You found him?" said Dyer brusquely.

"Yes. I come in for nine. My office is at the back of the house. I have my own key, so I took my coat off, changed my shoes, and switched my PC on before I went through to his study. I knocked but he didn't respond, so I looked in, and saw him, just like he is now. I phoned the police right away."

"Okay. So how are these bottles organised?" Dyer gestured at the cabinets.

"You've not read *Mapping the Taste of Scotland* then? That's Steven's most popular book. Onto its fifth edition now."

"We cops don't get a lot of time to read. Just tell me how it works."

"The shelves follow Steven's whisky map. It's quite simple. Heavy at the bottom, light at the top, and then left to right by taste, so the smokier ones at the left, and the more floral ones towards the right."

"So this Dalpittrie, where would that be?"
She thought for a moment
"Second shelf down, two or three in from the right. The cabinet's not locked."
Dyer opened the rightmost cabinet and examined the bottles on the second shelf down. He took down the third from the end. "Hah! Here it is. An Islay. I was right. The bottles were switched."
"Which one is it?" asked Ms Stanton.
Dyer showed her the bottle. "How do you say this?"
"Ah, Baile a Tuath." She repeated slowly, "That's 'Baaly a too-ah.'"
"What does it mean?" asked Clements.
"Northern township or settlement. The distillery's at the north end of Islay. And the bottle's definitely in the wrong place. You know your whisky, inspector."
Dyer smiled smugly. "A man's drink," he repeated. "But why would the killer want to hide it?"
"Perhaps it gives away his name," suggested Clements.
"Northern township!" sneered Dyer, "I don't think so."
"You could shorten it. Norton, or something like that."
Ms Stanton looked surprised. "Norton, did you say?"
"Yes, why?"
"The company's sales manager is Gerald Norton."
"Could he have wanted McIlmer dead?" snapped Dyer.
"Well, there has been some difficulty. Money going missing. Steven, I mean Mr McIlmer, suspected he was dipping his hand in the till. He was going to fire Norton in the New Year. Maybe even report him to the police."
"He's our man!" announced Dyer. "Clear as crystal! Yes, he came to ask McIlmer not to sack him, then threatened him, finally lost patience and shot him. Then spotted the bottle, knew it would point to him."
"Steven always liked to offer visitors a whisky that somehow related to them," added Ms Stanton. "He would have explained the meaning of the name to Mr Norton."
"Good thing I spotted that switch," said Dyer. "Otherwise he'd have got away with it. Got an address for him?"
"I'll get it for you."

Five minutes later Dyer had the white suit off, and was ready to leave. "You stay here," he told Clements, "keep an eye on things. Anything else you can find about Norton, email me. Now," he announced to no-one in particular, "I'll nail that bastard. Let the hunt begin!"

Ms Stanton stood by the balustrade at the front of the decking, and watched the inspector's car drive down the hill and turn onto the road to Perth. DC Clements joined her.

"Good work, Ann," said Ms Stanton, "I think it worked. Your tip-off on Saturday that the others were off was crucial. Dyer had to bring you with him."

"What if Norton has an alibi?"

"He won't. I used a pay-as-you-go phone to text him, from 'a friend,' saying I knew about his embezzlement, and I'd meet him on Sunday evening at five at the Royal Hotel in Comrie, 'to discuss terms.' That's the time I shot Steven. I never went to the hotel. Norton did, sent a 'Where are you?' text. Plenty of witnesses will have seen him, near here, at the right time. In any case, they'll never find Norton. The address I gave Dyer was five years out of date, from just after his divorce. I replied to Norton's text, saying it was too dangerous to meet, the cops were onto him. He'll be out of the country by now. He's got a bolt-hole in France, a cottage in the foothills of the Jura."

"Did you get rid of the phone?"

"Smashed it up, flushed the SIM card down the loo, put the rest in a litter bin in Crieff."

"Was McIlmer onto him?"

"Oh yes. But once he started nosing around, he'd have checked his rare whisky collection down in the basement, and noticed some gaps. A good few bottles are now in my room in a secure self-storage facility in Glasgow. But now he's dead, no-one will challenge the new inventory of the collection that I've prepared."

"So what now?"

"Stick to the plan. Resign in a couple of months. Then we'll move abroad. Germany. Start a company offering whisky tours, there's huge demand there. And we'll get a lot for the rare whiskies I acquired, even if we sell it quietly. And, of course, we can get married."

They looked at each other, and time slowed down. The kiss was brief, but seemed to last a lifetime.

A white-suited figure observed that moment through the study window. But Thing Two knew better than to get involved in anything other than forensics. Besides which, she believed that tenderness was a virtue often overlooked.

A Letter from America

Twenty years ago, not long before he died, an old uncle gave me a big cardboard box labelled 'Family History.' We'd visited him regularly and he knew I was interested in our family's past. Demands of work and home prevented me from doing much with that stuff, but recently, with the children out of the nest, and work scaled down to part-time, I got down to the business of going through it. Amongst the papers, envelopes, old driving licences, address books, and photograph albums was a cigar box tied shut with string. Inside were several letters and postcards, all addressed to Catherine Forgie, at her home in Dundee, and sent between 1881 and 1899. Catherine Forgie was my uncle's great-grandmother, thus my great-great-grandmother; she was born in 1834 and died in 1902. This letter was the most interesting item in the box; it was written by her niece Charlotte Davie, who had left Scotland as a child, with her family, to settle in the USA.

Dunkirk, New York, 15 April 1883

Dear Aunt Katie

I know it's a while since I wrote you, things have not been easy since then. I didn't want to write until life settled down a bit. Last time I wrote I was in Pittsburgh, and you know I had a hard time there. Dunkirk is so much nicer, a small town by the lake. There's something good about being near water, isn't there? That's what I remember about Scotland, we were always near the water.

But things never go the way you think, do they?

Not long after I got here, I was lucky to find a position. There was an old lady, Mrs. Delarge, who had a big old house on the edge of town. She couldn't see so well any more and wanted someone to come every afternoon and read to her. I thought it might be the Bible or some tedious old stuff. But no, she enjoyed books with a bit of excitement (I don't mean to suggest the Bible's no exciting, Auntie). Charles Dickens, Wilkie Collins, and so on. Have you read Mrs Green's books? I don't suppose you can get them over there, but they're very popular here. The Leavenworth Case was so gripping. Mrs. Delarge ordered them from a bookseller in Chicago. He sent two new books each month. She also got me to read the short stories they print in the newspaper, as well as the main news items. I guess I'm a lot more educated now than when I arrived. And know a lot more about what's happening in the world too. I think that's where she lived her life, in the words on the page.

Mrs. Delarge seemed to like my reading. 'Talking ink, that's what you are, child,' she said to me once. Fancy being called a child at twenty-three. It made me feel young.

After a few weeks she asked me if I'd like to stay in her house. I said to her thanks but no thanks. To be honest, apart from her choice in reading, I didn't like her that much. She was one of those old ladies who's always finding fault with folk. She wasn't so bad with me, I must admit. But I was only there four hours a day, and she thought I did the reading fine, even said she liked my accent. But her poor maid, a wee Irish girl called Brigid, she made her life, well, I won't say the word, Auntie, but you ken what it is. And made her work all hours. I knew if I lived in, she'd do the same with me. I like my freedom. My lodgings were neat, and I had time to myself. What she paid me was meagre, but enough to keep me going. And I got meals there too, lunch when I arrived, tea before I left, so I didn't need to do much by way of cooking. Except Sunday. Mrs. Delarge would have employed me seven days in the week. But I wanted one day off.

The old lady was suspicious of folk too, always thought they were after cheating her. Maybe that was from reading all those novels about robbers, swindlers and such. She said to me once she had lots of money, and folks was always trying to trick her out of it. She'd argue every bill a tradesman gave her, so that most of them wouldn't come to the house to work there any more. Which was real needful, as the roof leaked and some of the windows didn't shut proper. She just didn't like spending money. Except on books, I guess.

Enter the captain, as Shakespeare says. Captain Bencher, that's what he said his name was, anyhow. He came to the door, offered to fix the windows. His price must have been cheap, for she took him on. He told me he'd been master of a ship that sailed the seven seas, and right enough, he knew of lands I'd never heard of, not even read of in Mrs. Delarge's newspaper. He looked the part too, all weather-beaten, with a big scar across his forehead. When I asked him, he said he got it from a whale, the story was real exciting. But another time, he must have forgot – the story was the same but it was a shark instead.

He also had a Chinese girl who helped him with the work – he called her his concubine. Her name was Hwo Lin. She didn't speak English so well, but she was fair nice, I took to her right away, we were soon good friends. I never knew the captain's first name, Lin always called him 'captain,' so I did too. Charley's what he always called me, even though I told him I didn't like it, it sounded too common.

There was plenty of work for him. Once he'd fixed the windows, he started on the roof. But Mrs. Delarge was always suspicious of him. She told me once she wished the windows hadn't needed fixing, cause it gave him the excuse to walk all through the house, wherever he wanted. She reckoned he was looking for the place she kept her money hid. "But," she said, "he ain't ever going to find it. Not in a hundred years." Then she laughed, a sharp, rasping sort of laugh. She didn't do that too often.

The captain was indeed convinced there was a pot of money hidden somewhere in the house. He even asked me once if I could persuade the old lady to tell me where it was – "she seems to trust you," he said, "We could split it between us."

But I wasn't having it. "You get on with your own dirty business," I told him. He wasn't so happy with that, didn't speak to me for a while.

One day Mrs. Delarge said to me, real sweet like, "I want you to know, child, that I've left you some of my money, so that if I die, you'll see yourself all right." I didn't know what to make of that, you'd not say generosity was one of her virtues. I guess I should say what were her virtues, punctuality I suppose, and a love of books.

I mentioned it to the captain and Lin – that's what we called Hwo Lin – when we went for a picnic one Sunday by the lake shore. He was very impressed. "You've won her over, that's for sure," was his comment. "If she were to cop it, you'd be a rich girl all right. The old bird's got no children, you know." Well, I didn't consider it were proper to dwell on that sort of thing. We receive what the Lord gives us, after all. So no more was said on the matter.

My life here was fine, but soon it was all shook up again. One morning, about two weeks later, poor Brigid found Mrs. Delarge dead in her bed. The doctor was called – Doctor Kleist, he was German – and he thought she'd had a heart attack, or a congestion of the chest. Because her death was sudden and unexpected – I'd never known her to be other than in perfect health – the county coroner was called in. His name was Byers, a real gentleman too. We all had to wait in the kitchen – Brigid, the captain, Lin and myself. Then Mr. Byers talked to us, one at a time, in the drawing-room, about what happened. Brigid was the first in, then the captain, and then Lin. I guess they were each sent off afterwards so they didn't talk to those who were waiting. I was the last in.

Mr. Byers wanted to know what everyone working for her was doing on the night of Mrs. Delarge's death. Had we seen anyone doing anything odd or suspicious? Me, I'd gone a walk along the shore, then early to bed, so I'd not seen anything much, odd or not. Mr. Byers asked me all about what the captain was doing in the house, and if I'd ever seen him doing anything funny. "Well, no," I said, "not really, not apart from his work, that is." He went on to ask similar questions about Brigid and even Lin. I did my best to answer honestly, that there was no reason I had to suspect anyone of anything. He asked me not to leave town, and gave me five dollars, "so that I should not be out of pocket," he said.

I didn't see the captain and Lin until the following morning. I was taking my walk by the shore when I met them.

"What did you tell old Byers?" the captain wanted to know.

"Well, nothing but the truth," I said. "What else should I say?"

"I reckon he's on to me," he whispered. "I dunno why, either, I was real careful."

I couldn't believe what I was hearing, Auntie, I didn't know what to say. I must have looked daft, just gaping at him.

"That's right," he said. "I killed the old bird. Stifled her with the pillow. But I was real careful, I tell you. No footprints in the mud outside the house, wiped my hands beforehand too, so's there'd be no dirt on the pillow. I don't know why Byers is asking so many questions. Did you tell him anything?"

I was stunned, I can tell you. "Why did you do it?" was all I could say.

"Isn't it obvious?" He was kind of pleading with me to understand him. "For the money, of course. You'd get all that loot, and you'd share it with us. We're your pals after all. I've made you rich, Charley."

"I don't want to be rich," I replied. That wasn't strictly true, I'd love to be rich, in fact. But from doing something worthwhile, something that people appreciate. Not by killing folks.

"Well," he said, "You are, and that's that. If you don't want the money, you can give it to us. We can always use a dollar or two."

I worried something terrible after that. But there were no more questions from Mr. Byers.

However, a few days later, I got a note at my lodgings asking me to go to his office on Main Street at two o'clock that afternoon. I put on my best clothes. "Always dress your best for the minister or the lawyer," my Granny used to say when I was little. I even put on my kid gloves, the ones you sent over for my eighteenth birthday. They were beautiful, so fine, so smooth.

When I arrived, I was surprised to find the captain and Lin already in the waiting room. The captain looked grim, Lin as always seemed calm. She seemed able to ride all of life's storms with a composure that was inside her, if you see what I mean. Then the three of us were called into Mr Byers' inner sanctum. He rose from his great oaken desk to greet us, asked us very politely to sit down.

"I'm wearing two hats today," he began. "My first is that of the county coroner. As such, I can tell you that the inquiry into

Mrs. Delarge's death has been completed. It's been concluded that, on the balance of probabilities, Mrs. Delarge's death was natural. It was probably caused by a sudden congestion of the lungs leading to asphyxiation."

"You said probably," I asked, without thinking. "Was there something not quite right?" I noticed the captain stiffen.

"In such cases," explained Mr. Byers, "there is always room for alternative explanations. The situation has been complicated by the fact that Miss Brigid Kelly has disappeared, along with some items of jewellery and silverware. Inevitably the question arises, whether Miss Kelly brought about Mrs. Delarge's demise – for instance, by suffocating her with a pillow or scarf – with the intent of robbery. Or whether she simply took advantage of Mrs. Delarge's sudden death, from entirely natural causes, to help herself to some valuables. There is however, at present no evidence to sustain the former hypothesis. Naturally, when we find Miss Kelly, we shall be raising some questions."

I saw the captain relax. Brigid had, by a minor misdemeanour, attracted to herself the clear suspicion of a capital offence. Although softly spoken, Mr. Byers' implication was clear – when Brigid was caught, she could hang.

"I'm sure Brigid wouldn't do violence on anyone," I said. "It's not her nature."

"We'll see," said Mr. Byers, looking at me closely. Then he leaned back and smiled. "Now I have to take off my coroner's hat, and revert to Old Byers the lawyer. Except that I happen to be Mrs. Delarge's lawyer. And in that capacity I have some business with you."

I noticed the captain sit up and pay attention. "All three of us?" he asked.

"That's correct," said Mr. Byers, as friendly as you like. "All three of you are addressed in Mrs. Delarge's will." He opened the top right hand drawer of his mighty desk, and extracted a bundle tied with red ribbon. He carefully untied the ribbon and separated out four long brown envelopes, which he laid side by side on the desk.

"There is one of these for each of you," he said. He examined the writing on the first, and pushed it aside. "Sadly Miss Kelly is not here, hers must therefore wait." He slid the next envelope across the desk to me, then one to Lin. "Ladies first," he said politely. And finally one to the captain. He cleared his throat, and assumed a solemn expression. I smiled at his play-acting, and he looked away.

"You are required, under the terms of Mrs. Delarge's testament, to examine and read the contents of your envelope here and now, in my presence. Then you may ask any questions. I will do my best to answer, but I am not aware of the contents. These letters were prepared by Mrs. Delarge herself some weeks before she passed on. You may all do it together. It is up to yourselves whether you let me see them. He passed the paper knife round so that we could each slit open the envelope.

I extracted a single sheet of heavy and shiny legal paper, and saw that it was covered with writing on one side. I recognised the hand as that of Mrs. Delarge; it was an italic style, favoured many years ago in schools, but, though the letters were large, it was not easy to make out. Nevertheless, I was familiar with her writing and so began to read.

No sooner had I started, than I noticed a black smudge on the middle finger of my right glove, and drew my hand quickly away from the paper. I realised Mrs. Delarge had used a heavy ink on paper too shiny to absorb it well, and much of it, although dry, remained on the surface of the paper. I could have taken off my glove, but, judging that would not have been ladylike in the company of Mr. Byers, I took the alternative course of holding the paper by the edges, making sure that my fingers did not stray from the margins.

Glancing at the others, I noticed that the captain, for whom cleanliness was less of an instinct, running his fingertips, already blackened, along the line of text as he read, slowly and with difficulty, muttering the words to himself. Lin had simply laid the paper before her on the desk. It was clear to me that she couldn't read a word of it. I touched her arm and said, "Don't worry, Lin, I'll read yours to you once I've read mine. You just wait a wee moment." She smiled her thanks, and I read on.

I must admit, Auntie, I had a fair shock. When I'd seen the

envelopes, I'd thought Mrs. Delarge, in contemplating her future arrival at the gates of Heaven, had left to each of us a modest sum. But what I read was a ranting diatribe of accusations. She claimed that I, "no doubt in collusion with others," was intent on stealing her valuables and cash, contemplating perhaps even murder. She had observed various signs and indications, which she declined to specify, but assured me that we would not succeed in carrying to completion our intentions against her. She concluded "If you are reading this text, then you have implemented your murderous plans. Yet you shall not escape the punishment due. You will face the Almighty's verdict at the Day of Judgement, but my vengeance will come before that. You may rest assured of it."

Mrs. Delarge had never said anything like this to me. Yet it was in character with her distrustful nature, especially towards those she judged her social inferiors. I resolved not to let it bother me, and put the letter back on the table without a word.

Now I took up Lin's epistle. I asked her first if she had no objection to Mr. Byers hearing its contents, to which suggestion she was agreeable. I felt neither I nor Lin had anything to hide, and if Mr. Byers knew Mrs. Delarge well enough, he would not be surprised at the letter's content.

And so it turned out. The outpouring of spite directed at Lin was very similar to mine, employing many of the same sentences, and with the same threats, with the addition of some very unpleasant references to Lin's oriental origins. Mr. Byers nodded gravely as I read, while Lin struggled to understand what was being said. "By Jove," shouted the captain, interrupting my reading, "mine's just the same. Sure, the old dame's a crackpot. The least she could have done was given us a few dollars for all we did for her. After all, we're the innocent parties. It's that Irish hussy who's done for her."

Mr. Byers merely stared blandly at the captain. Once I had finished reading, he said, rather sadly I thought, "Yes, I suppose I was expecting something like that." He leaned back, so that his chair creaked, and went on after a moment. "Well, now that's done, I should tell you of Mrs. Delarge's will. In fact, there's not much to tell, she had very few assets. The house is mortgaged to the bank. In fact, it was at their insistence that she had the windows and roof repaired. She had shares in a railroad, but it went bankrupt some years ago. She had bonds also, but cashed them to fund the house repairs, and her burial. Her few valuables have vanished along with Miss Kelly. All that's left are her clothes, books and furniture. They are worth next to nothing."

He looked directly at me then. "But since I know, Miss Davie, from what Mrs. Delarge told me, that you are a lover of books yourself, I, as her executor, am happy that you take any of the books you wish. I must confess that I've already taken one or two which are of interest to myself. Perhaps you would come around to the house tomorrow at ten. My clerk will meet you and note the volumes you choose, purely a legal formality which will have no consequences to yourself. He will also help convey them to your lodgings."

He stood up abruptly. "Thank you all for coming in. I'll bid you good day now." Being a courteous man, he shook hands with each of us. The captain, seeing his fingers dark with ink, hastily licked them clean and wiped them on his already grubby handkerchief. Mr. Byers shook hands with him politely, for which I admired him, but I have no doubt but that as soon as we were off his premises, he washed his hands very thoroughly. I would have done the same. We left the letters behind, for there seemed little point in retaining them.

The next morning I came across the captain and Lin by the shore again, sitting on a bench facing the lake. The captain did not look well. He agreed that he wasn't feeling quite right. I asked to see his tongue, and noted the dark colouration. I advised him to see the doctor at once.

"Bah, I've had worse than this at sea," he grumped, and produced from his pocket a half-bottle of Kentucky whiskey. After a few swigs he put the bottle down, took out his handkerchief and coughed some thick black fluid onto it. The stain on the grimy cloth looked like the jellyfish we used to see on the beach when I was little, but smaller, and black as ink, quivering as if about to jump away from him. I guess that was his hand shaking.

By the next morning he was dead. Doctor Kleist, being called to certify the death, suspected he had died of consuming some poisonous matter. When Lin came over to tell me, I immediately thought of the letter from Mrs. Delarge, and the inky stains on the captain's fingers.

I was not alone in my suspicion. Mr. Byers, as coroner, had sent the letters from Mrs. Delarge to Buffalo for chemical analysis. The ink contained, as I think you will already suspect, Auntie, generous amounts of an alkaloid substance used sparingly as a heart stimulant, but in large doses inevitably fatal. Although normally taken by mouth, it could be easily absorbed through the skin. The shiny paper had, of course, been chosen for its poor quality of absorption. It seemed the captain had been killed by the woman whom he himself had murdered.

Brigid has not reappeared, I don't suppose she ever will. Lin and I are planning to leave Dunkirk soon. We'll go further west now, to California if we can. I'll write again in a few weeks.

I hope you're well.

With all good wishes, Charlotte.

There were other letters in the box from Charlotte, but none of them contains any further reference to these events. I did however find out more of the history of Miss Davie. She and Hwo Lin formed a close, perhaps intimate, relationship, and moved together to Los Angeles, where they lived together for the remainder of their lives. Charlotte Davie submitted stories to the Los Angeles Herald, and subsequently became a successful writer of detective fiction, in the manner of Anna Katherine Green or Robert Barr. She died in 1934. Linda Hwo, as Lin later called herself, achieved minor fame as a sculptor, and died in 1937. Curiously, I had, amongst the crowded shelves in my study, a couple of volumes which I believe came down to me by the same uncle who gave me the box of letters. They are both by Charlotte Davie, The Epistle of Doom *and* A Warning in Black Letters.

The Prize

I coveted the Stangerson Prize as soon as I saw the announcement. There wasn't much detail, so I contacted my agent.

"It's a bit controversial, Mandy," she said.

"But ten grand, Emmy, that's a lot of money. And a bronze heron thrown in. I can put up with controversy for that. What's it all about, anyway?"

"The prize is awarded by the Stangerson Trust for a novel set in Scotland. The trust was endowed by Yevgeny Stangerson, a Russian billionaire. There was a piece in the paper about him recently. He was just a party official until an all-night drinking session with Boris Yeltsin in 1992, from which he emerged with a mineral concession for a third of Siberia."

"And a hangover, I'll bet!"

"Hmm. Like many of these nouveaux riches, he was desperate for some class, and commissioned a genealogical agency to trace his family tree in the hope something impressive would come up. They weren't stupid, and delivered what was required, joining up some dodgy connections and inventing others. Stangerson thinks he's descended from a Scottish nobleman who served the Czar in the 1660s and was made a Count of the Russian Empire. Now he calls himself Count Stangerson. He was told his family's origins are in the village of Stonehouse in Lanarkshire, and that Stangerson is a corruption of Stonehouse. So he set up the trust and the prize, to pay tribute to his roots."

"Well, I can't disagree with any of that. What's the problem?"

"The problem is that Yevgeny isn't the best friend of our environment. They reckon his mining operations have polluted 200,000 square miles of the Siberian tundra. He's even personally shot three Siberian tigers. Then there's his investments: fracking, tobacco, alcohol, weapons, pharmaceuticals; he's into all of them. Oh, and there's the allegations about dodgy financial dealings, you know, money laundering, tax avoidance, fake charities, the usual. Do you want any more? Most of the big authors won't go near the prize in case people stop buying their books."

"That's not a problem for me. Anyway, I write romances, who's going to boycott them? And I need the money."

"Okay Mandy, I'll see what I can do. I may have a bit of leverage with one of the judges. Meanwhile, you should ask your publishers to enter your most recent book. That's *The Barren Fields Shall Bloom*, isn't it? I'll have a little word with them too."

The publishers, Flat Hedgehog Press, were only too happy to enter me. So happy that I wondered whether Emmy had got to them first. Then it was a question of waiting. The trouble with these literary prizes is that no-one has any idea how the winners are picked. In this case, the Stangerson Trust's website proclaimed that "a carefully chosen panel of expert readers, two hundred in all, located in all parts of Scotland as well as the USA, Canada, Australia and New Zealand, will read the entries and rate them according to a set of objective criteria prepared by scientists at the Stangerson Institute in St. Petersburg." But no sign of the 'objective criteria' themselves.

So I was left to agonise over whether *The Barren Fields Shall Bloom* would make the grade. It was the fourth novel I'd had published, and I felt that the plot was particularly strong. Zoe McTavish, a primary school teacher in her early twenties, working at a school in the poorer end of Coatbridge, inherits, from an aged aunt, a cottage in the Highlands of Scotland, not far from romantic Loch Maree. Having been told by a Romany fortune-teller at a local fair that, "You must seek out barren land, there love will blossom," she gives up her teaching job and moves to the cottage, intending to set up a pottery and subsist by crofting. But the cottage and croft are almost derelict, and it takes more money than she had planned for to set up the pottery. Things are not looking good, when a handsome man buys a tasteful vase from her. He is Rory McTurk, currently involved in a complex legal battle to gain his inheritance, a substantial estate and the title of Earl of Gairloch. I won't go into detail, in case you read it, but you can see the drift. I think it's rather good, although reviews have been a bit varied, from 'absolutely sublime' to 'preposterous shite.' Mind you, I think the latter was written by another author – the League of Romancers is all gush on the surface, but there are some pretty bitchy scribblers lurking underneath.

Anyway, to cut a long story short – and I'm reluctant to leave out the anguished episodes of that two month wait – at last I got an email from Julian Humbridge of the Stangerson Trust Literary Committee to tell me I'd been shortlisted. I can't tell you how pleased I was. At last I was recognised. But not there yet; the prize beckoned. "You're on your own now," said Emmy. What was she talking about? I wasn't going to let it go now I was so close.

The first thing to do was examine the competition. The only one of the other three shortlistees I'd heard of was Walter Kellastoun: his genre historical fiction, his shortlisted volume *The Beckoning Dark*, a dramatisation of the last days of King Alexander III. Carina Spolther, I found from Wikipedia, is Professor of Creative Writing at the University of Southern Scotland; her entry was *Herrings on my Clothesline*, an account of an imagined visit by a dysfunctional middle-class family to a holiday cottage in Shetland. And finally, Edwina Jakubek, whose crime novel *My Art is All Things* features the hunt for a serial killer who stuffs his (or her) victims and sets up the thus-preserved corpses as artistic exhibits during the Edinburgh Festival.

I obtained all three. *The Beckoning Dark* was only available in hardback, but my local library were happy to order it for me. *Herrings on my Clothesline* I found at a reasonable price on eBay. And *My Art is All Things* was already on sale as an eBook on Amazon for 99p. Now to read them.

My Art is All Things I read first, as it was instantly available. 'The Amazon Bestseller' it said at the beginning. But I wasn't impressed. The italicised thoughts of the killer told me right away that he was a complete crackpot with no basis in any recognisable reality. The plot was completely implausible, and his stuffing technique didn't equate with any of the information on taxidermy I found on the web. Similarly, the casual ignorance of the policeman, admittedly drunk most of the time, did not match the careful scrutiny I had incurred for speeding on the A9. 'I coulda been a contender,' said Marlon Brando in *On The Waterfront*. As far as the prize was concerned, this book wasn't.

Later that week, *Herrings on my Clothesline* dropped through the letterbox. The cover was pink and yellow, with cartoon kippers pegged to a clothesline, against a seaside backdrop that revealed the illustrator had never been near Shetland. I struggled my way through the glutinous prose, heavy with forced metaphors and self-consciously poetic utterances, and tried to work out what the hell was going on. Though well-known spots were mentioned, the descriptions had all the detail you get on Wikipedia, but no real sense of place. The Lerwick portrayed seemed more like North Berwick. Which, coincidentally, is where Professor Spolther lives. No, I didn't think this pretentious gloop would challenge me.

It was another week before I got an email from the library that *The Beckoning Dark* had arrived. I plunged into it immediately, and from that moment was utterly gripped. A growing sense of foreboding hangs over Alexander as he returns from Edinburgh to Fife against the advice of his courtiers. He hurries to see his new young wife, the only hope for his dynasty after all three of his children have died. And in the dark, a stumble of his horse on the steep bank above the beach at Kinghorn, pitches Scotland into chaos. I read it in two days. And it was clear that this book would win the prize.

I am aware of my literary limitations. And here I had been brought to face them. After the hope that sprang up within me as I read the first two books, I now knew that winning the prize must be a practical rather than a literary accomplishment. Although I knew immediately that Kellastoun's was the likely winner, it was also just possible that even *Herrings* and *My Art* might stand a chance, depending on the judges. These things were so subjective.

So I set to work. First I studied the list of judges. This was no help. An agent, a publisher, a journalist, a psychologist and a crime writer. There was no telling which way they'd jump. It was even possible the whole thing was set up, and the winner already decided. Nevertheless, I'm not one to turn away from a challenge. So next I studied the rules. Very carefully.

The first rule that caught my attention was Rule 15b, which defined exactly what 'set in Scotland' meant. The rule required

80% of the action of the novel to take place within Scotland itself. My own book passed this test with flying colours, but did the others? *The Beckoning Dark* was set entirely in Scotland, along Alexander's route from Edinburgh Castle to his intended destination at Kinghorn Castle. *Herrings on my Clothesline* included a prologue in which the family, in their Victorian flat in some gentrified zone of London, discuss the forthcoming trip. I began an eager wordcount. But at 6,700 words out of 84,000, the English part of the book was well within the guidelines. *My Art is All Things* has lengthy monologues by the supposed killer. On re-reading the book I realised only on page 346 that this person is for most of the book confined in a mental hospital near Carlisle. A furious wordcount revealed 22,100 words of the 'Carlisle monologues' in a book of 105,000 words. Twenty-one percent!

There was no way I was going to raise this publicly myself; it wouldn't do my image any good at all. However, I soon hired a lawyer who wrote to the publishers of *My Art is All Things* on behalf of an anonymous client, saying that in the event of the book winning the prize, their cheating would be made public. The letter was copied to the Stangerson Trust. Six days later Edwina Jakubek announced that she had asked her publishers to withdraw the book from the competition, as she could not condone Mr Stangerson's support of fracking. My chances of winning the prize had just got eight per cent better!

Now I noticed Rule 22d, which stipulated that the shortlistees must attend in person the award ceremony, to take place at the Lifestyles Leisure Centre in Stonehouse on the first Saturday in October. In five weeks' time. Non-attendees would be regarded as having withdrawn from the competition. This gave me an idea. I studied all I could find about my two remaining competitors. It's amazing what people will give away in terms of personal information about themselves to celebrity magazines. In an interview with *Celebrity Woman* magazine, Carina Spolther described her house in North Berwick in such detail that I could find it on Google Earth. The third house on the right along a street lined by large detached houses, possibly built in the 1930's. Large back gardens, with a lane running along the back, giving access to the garages. Carina also confessed that she was devoted to her three cats, her only companions there. "I'd do anything for them," she gushed. I wondered.

It's amazing what you can buy online. Two weeks later I was armed with a pistol, powered by compressed air, that fired paint pellets, along with a box of pellets of bright purple. I'd practised out in the country to get used to the weapon. I chose a day on which I knew Carina had an event in Edinburgh. Luckily it was warm and sunny. Sporting baggy clothes and a woolly hat that covered my hair completely, I strolled down the back lane, keeping close to the six-foot hedges that enclosed the rear gardens. However, each house had a double gate leading onto the lane, probably for vehicle access. Peeping from the lane over the gate into Carina's garden, I saw I was really in luck. A big fat ginger tom curled up asleep in the sun on the decking which ran along the rear of the house. I got in two shots as it jumped up and forced its overfed middle through the cat flap in the back door. Then I was off.

I'd been able to download for free some software that, if you typed in words, would read them out in a bland American accent. As there was no emphasis applied to any word, the sentences sounded stilted and unreal. Just what I needed. Here's what I typed in: 'This time purple pellets, next time real bullets. If you want the cats to live, exit the Stangerson.' I recorded the statement on my digital voice-recorder. I used a cheap and anonymous pay-as-you-go mobile to phone Carina – her number I found in a database maintained by The Association of Literary Authors – and play the clip to her voicemail. Ten minutes later I did it again; again it went to voicemail. The third time I heard it ring, Carina snatched up the phone. "Who the hell are you? What do you want? Leave my cats alone, do you hear!" I just played the recording again, and rang off. Three days later, Carina's publisher announced that she had withdrawn from the Stangerson Book Prize. The reason given was her disapproval of Stangerson's poor attitude to wildlife. I thought that was quite amusing.

Two down, one to go. And Walter Kellastoun had to go. Otherwise he would win. My studies of his magazine and newspaper interviews told me he was an obstinate old man who wouldn't give in to threats of any kind. And he didn't have any cats or dogs. I could have threatened to murder his wife, but that would likely have brought the police into things. However, I did learn one very useful thing: each morning about seven he was wont to take a walk from his house in Lamlash, Arran, along the steep cliff path overlooking the sea which led up and over the ridge and down towards Brodick.

I got myself to Arran a week later, two weeks before the award ceremony, on an evening ferry. I paid cash, gave a false name, wore a baseball cap, sat in one of the aircraft seats and read a book all the way. I brought sandwiches and a flask of coffee, and slept in the car. At 6.45 the next morning I parked on some waste ground at the top of the hill, just before the road runs down into Lamlash. Low cloud and drizzle reduced visibility nicely. I waited on the path, again in my baggy disguise, armed only with a copy of *The Beckoning Dark*. After a while I saw him coming up the path, in a blue waterproof jacket, a flat cap keeping the rain off his head, staring at the path through thick glasses, paying no attention to the precipitous drop onto the rocks on his right. Only a thin kerb of slightly raised turf separated the path from empty space.

As he came up to me, he looked at me suspiciously. I thrust forward the book. "Please, Mr Kellastoun," I wheedled, in a fake American accent, "your book is just wonderful. Will you sign it for me? I'd just love that so much." I held out also, in my gloved hand, a cheap biro. "Oh, alright," he grumbled, and took the pen. I held the book open at the title page, and as he leaned forward I pulled it back and gave him a hard shove. It pushed him sideways, so he couldn't simply stagger back, but tripped immediately in the raised turf kerb, and went over the edge. I peeped over to make sure he wasn't clinging to a branch. No, he was lying spread-eagled on the rocks far below, looking pretty dead. I made off rapidly, and was on the next ferry off the island. Job done. Now all I had to do was turn up and collect the prize.

Kellastoun's body was found later that day. The police were called as a matter of routine. But what would they find? There was nothing to link him to me. Except the Stangerson Prize.

The next two weeks I have to say I was really on edge. But I heard nothing from anyone investigating the death. What I noticed was that the literary world heaped praise on Edwina and Carina for their 'principled stand' against Stangerson's dodgy activities. They became celebrities, and sales of their books shot up. Who cares about the quality – feel the fame! On top of that, glowing appreciations of Walter Kellastoun appeared in all the Sunday supplements – the greatest writer of historical fiction since Robert Louis Stevenson, and sure-fire winner of the Stangerson Prize, if only death had not snatched it from his hands. Now, they concluded, the prize would fall – fall! – by default to the only writer left in the running. They didn't even mention my name. And, of course, sales of Walter's books – even ones long forgotten – rocketed. Not that he would benefit personally.

One of the Kellastoun pieces even suggested 'the remaining writer in the contest' should do the decent thing and withdraw as a tribute to Walter Kellastoun. The next day Emmy phoned, to suggest withdrawing might be a good idea, in view of how it would be received by the reading public. I normally do just what she tells me. She knows the market and always suggests what will make more money for me and for herself. This time I refused. I'd never won a prize, and I wasn't going to let this one go. She didn't argue, but I could tell she wasn't pleased.

I was duly invited to the award ceremony, in Stonehouse. I even bought a new frock for the event. I don't know that part of the country, so it took a while for my SatNav to get me there, and I arrived just ten minutes before the start. I was met at the door by Terry McGeachan, a minor presenter on Radio Clydesdale. "So glad you made it, darling" he gushed insincerely. "After all, you're the last man standing." I didn't laugh.

He led me down a long corridor to the double doors leading into the auditorium, at the heart of the complex. As we entered, I got a shock. A huge picture of Walter Kellastoun hung over the stage. "Yes," breezed Terry, "we decided that we needed to celebrate poor Walter. After all, he didn't pull out, like those other two. I'll tell you a secret. Their books were nothing, smoke and mirrors, no substance. You and Walt were the only two in it. You'll get the prize, of course, but we couldn't just ignore his sad passing, just as fame was beckoning him." He showed me to a table just below the stage. Emmy was already there, looking uncomfortable. There were two bottles of wine and she was already well into one of them.

I glanced around. I recognised quite a few of the people at the other tables. Agents, a few publishers, someone from the Caledonian Book Trust, a few tabloid journalists, a tableful of book bloggers, some other authors, none of them well-known, presumably hoping to be seen or maybe just there for the free booze. Plenty of others I didn't know, including several men in business suits. Were they Russian? I couldn't say, that would be stereotyping, but they did look kind of similar, slightly overweight with crew cuts or shaven heads. Maybe the bottles of vodka on their table were significant.

No-one else arrived at our table, and the event got under way. Terry welcomed everyone and introduced Donald Scarpov, the Chair of the Stangerson Trust. One of the men at the table with vodka stood up, encompassed most of the audience with a sweep of his hand, as if including them all in a blessing, then sat down again.

Terry now explained that Walter Kellastoun's untimely passing hung like a shadow over this year's prize award, and could not be ignored. He invited veteran actor Edgar Monckthwaite onto the stage to offer a eulogy to Walter. "I come to praise old Walter, not to bury him," he announced in plummy tones. The response showed how few were familiar with Shakespeare. What followed I can only describe as utterly shameless crawling to a man who was not there to receive it. Every superlative spewed forth, every overripe and drooling metaphor dragged up from forgotten thesauri was slathered forth in praise of Walter Kellastoun. And not a word of it sincere. It was truly sickening. And yet also a bravura performance from an actor of the old school.

Finally he paused, wiped his hand across his mouth, and looked down at me, then swept the rest of the hall in his gaze. "Mandy here," he said in tones rich and authoritative, and at this point a spotlight caught me in its dazzling grasp. "Mandy here stands to receive the Stangerson Prize for Scottish

Literature for 2017. But I appeal to her" – and with this he dropped to one knee and held his arms out in supplication – "I appeal to her to make an act of supreme sacrifice, to waive the award, in order that it can be laid by the tomb of Walter Kellastoun."

I was paralysed. I wasn't going to give up the prize, but everyone in that room was demanding it of me. I could feel it. I tried to think it through. This was what the emotion of the moment demanded, yet I knew that within five minutes attention would swing back to Walter Kellastoun, and I'd be nobody again. I gritted my teeth and stared back at Monckthwaite. It was like something out of silent movie. Everything stopped in the hall – talking, thinking, breathing. Time stood still.

Then Terry jumped to his feet. "A wonderful and deeply felt tribute, Edgar, supremely empathic, truly moving." He hung his head for a moment as if contemplating the rich legacy of Walter Kellastoun. "And I really do appreciate the deep emotion behind your proposal for a fitting tribute to our beloved Walter. But alas, the rules of the Stangerson Award are perfectly clear. It cannot be awarded to one who is no longer with us. If our shortlist were, by Amanda's noble sacrifice, to be reduced to zero, we simply cannot award the prize. And I cannot think that is what Walter would have wanted." He shook his head meaningfully. "No. But the Stangerson Trust is not deaf to the calls which you, Edgar, have brilliantly condensed and focused. And therefore I am happy, indeed, overjoyed, to announce that the Stangerson Trust has initiated a new award – The Stangerson Lifetime Award – to be awarded posthumously to an outstanding author who is cut short at the height of his or her powers. It will be available each year, but will only be awarded if there is a suitable candidate. And I am privileged to be able to announce that the very first Stangerson Lifetime Award will be made to Walter Kellastoun."

A wave of spontaneous and wild applause burst across the chamber. Cheers broke out, the audience leapt to its feet almost as one – I among them, for the sensation of relief took utter possession of me. I noticed one or two people openly weeping, and, whipping out a tissue, dabbed my eyes in sympathy. Terry produced a flat box about eight inches square, and opened it to display the large gold-plated disk bearing a profile in relief of Walter Kellastoun. The spotlight, which had moved away from me as soon as Terry had stood up to speak, now focused on Donald Scarpov who was now standing. He walked across to the stage, took the medal in its box from Terry, and walked over to a table at the rear of the hall. Here a woman dressed in black, whom I took to be Kellastoun's widow, stood shakily, supported by a dark-suited relative, to receive the award. Thunderous applause greeted the handover, following which Scarpov produced from his inside pocket an envelope which he handed to Mrs Kellastoun, with a few words which, owing to the noise, were inaudible.

I was right. After five minutes I had been forgotten. But now, almost as an afterthought, came the presentation of the Stangerson Prize for Scottish Writing. A young woman in an evening gown swept onto the stage bearing a large gold-coloured envelope. Terry announced her as Maxine Parmesan, and reminded us of her bit part in a fantasy epic, when she'd been eaten by a dragon. I remembered the scene: most of her clothes were artfully divested as the dragon shook her writhing body before swallowing her whole. It was still possible that, in a future series, she would be magically recovered.

"Who has won the award, Maxine?" announced Terry.

Maxine spent some time opening the envelope and pulling out a folded parchment. Finally she squinted at it – evidently she didn't wear her glasses on stage – and announced, "The winner of this year's Stangerson Award is...Amanda Swallow!" The applause was rather muted, this clearly being seen as an anticlimax, and I heard a certain amount of clinking as audience members took the opportunity to fill their glasses.

I acted surprised – who, me? – and mounted the stage to receive a hug and very sloppy kiss from Maxine, which, I later discovered, left a big smear of lipstick on my face. I could smell the gin on her breath as she gasped her congratulations. "I'm such an admirer of your work," she cooed.

But you've got to play the game. I whipped out my speech, to thank my parents, my teachers, my fellow writers, my agent and my publisher, "but mostly, I have to thank you, my readers, without whom I wouldn't be here tonight." Though I wondered how many of the audience here had actually read any of my books.

The response to my speech was perfunctory, as the waiters were already serving the avocado and prawn cocktail, the hungry literati gobbling it down as soon as it arrived. The rest of the evening was filled with the clatter of cutlery, the sounds of chewing, swallowing and slurping, and the endless yapping of trivial conversations. I was glad when it was over. But the object had been achieved: the Stangerson Award was mine!

My publishers were pleased too, and reprinted *The Barren Fields Shall Bloom* with a banner right across the front proclaiming the Award. Sales picked up too, though not as much as I had hoped.

Then another stroke of luck. Mrs Kellastoun admitted to a reporter that her husband, suffering from incurable cancer, had talked often of suicide. The idea that Kellastoun had fallen accidentally was rapidly supplanted by the assumption that he had killed himself.

But the next week it all turned bad. Yevgeny Stangerson was arrested in Los Angeles for tax fraud and money laundering. In Edinburgh, the offices of the Stangerson Trust in Queen Street were raided by police, and the office-bearers and staff rounded up for questioning. Except for Donald Scarpov, who, according to the newspapers, had left for Azerbaijan the previous day with two large suitcases.

Suddenly the Stangerson name was bad news. Flat Hedgehog Press pulped the whole reprint, then cancelled their contract with me for two more books. I was too closely associated with the prize, they said, and the circumstances of the award seemed to suggest I was set up to win. I needed to take some time out to let the dust settle, perhaps adopt a new *nom de plume*, and look at a different genre. I should get back to them in perhaps a couple of years.

Hot on their heels was Emmy, whose attitude towards me had changed as soon as I'd refused to withdraw from the contest. A brief letter from her office, signed by a secretary with a squiggle, informed me curtly that she no longer felt able to represent me.

I should, however, not belittle my moment of fame. After all, it enabled someone to recognise me as a fellow passenger on the Arran ferry. On the night before Walter Kellastoun died. What did they do with this information? Put it on social media of course. It aroused intense discussion. One or two reckoned I'd gone over to kill him, but this theory was considered far too melodramatic. The idea that gained ground was that he had summoned me to a secret meeting to tell me of his intention to end his life the next day. The fact that he fell clutching a pen was considered a coded message. The writer falls silent, the pen stops moving.

So I was ready for them, when a detective inspector and her heavy came calling. DI McClintock (little) and DC Smollett (large). She did the talking, he just grinned or frowned, more or less at random. I knew they'd have seen the tweets, and checked the CCTV at the ferry terminal, so I admitted immediately that I'd been over on Arran that night and returned the next morning.

"Why did you visit Arran?" she asked.

"It's a confidential matter. I'm not at liberty to say. I'm sorry."

"Did you go over to meet with Walter Kellastoun?" Had she fallen for that one?

I hesitated long enough for her to over-interpret my response. "No comment."

"What did you talk about?"

"I'm not at liberty to say."

"So you did meet him?"

"No comment."

Smollett suddenly interjected, "Did you kill him?"

"Good Lord, why would I do that? He was a great writer. Was that a joke?"

Smollett grinned, "Yeah."

"Alright, I promised him I'd not reveal this, but you've guessed most of it," I conceded reluctantly. "He asked me to meet him at the top of the hill at 7 o'clock. He told me he had cancer, he couldn't take it any longer, he was going to end it that day. He wished me luck in my career. He gave me a hug, and then he went off, and I drove down to the ferry. I cried on the way back. He was so sad." I dabbed my eye with a tissue.

They asked if they could borrow the clothes I was wearing then. I went through to the bedroom and rummaged about. Of course, I'd got rid of everything I was wearing as soon as I got back, jacket, shoes, jeans, underwear, the lot. But I had a complete set there for the cops. I'd worn them a bit too, so they weren't completely new. They gave me a receipt, put them in a clear plastic bag, and took them away. I didn't hear from them again.

Until I was summoned to attend the Fatal Accident Inquiry. I told the Sheriff just what I'd told the cops. The sheriff concluded that there were three possibilities: he'd fallen accidentally, he'd thrown himself off, or he'd been pushed. He ruled out murder as the least likely, although he admonished me for not coming forward earlier to reveal my meeting with the deceased. He also ruled out suicide, admitting there was some evidence for it, but that it was not conclusive. I suspect more in deference to the feelings of Mrs Kellastoun, he ruled in favour of accidental death. As I filed out of the courtroom, DC Smollett came up behind me. I could smell bacon on his breath. "You did it, didn't you?" he whispered. "I know it, and you know it. I won't forget it, that's my promise to you." Then he was gone.

That was five years ago. He's not as stupid as I thought. Now he's a detective inspector. But he's based in Aberdeen now, far away from me. I've managed to get by. I've a new name, and even a new *nom de plume*. Now I'm Gil Dempster, writer of gritty westerns. You may have come across *The Gulch my Grave* or *Bullets at Noon* or my most recent opus, *A Fast Draw can be Fatal.* I thought about entering that one for the Putin Prize for Western Fiction. But I'd have to turn up in Millport for the presentation. A bit too public. Best stay under the radar. Westerns are a living, but not a good one. I'm thinking about moving into science fiction. Or to Australia.

Music in the Night

Disposing of a piano is no easy matter. Our children had flown the nest, and, my income being unpredictable, Anne and I decided to downsize. That meant some things had to go. One of the items we identified was the piano, which stood against one of the dining room walls, and had been gifted to us by Anne's father when our children were young. Over a hundred years old, we'd been told, and made in France, it was a beautiful instrument with a wonderful tone. Kept regularly tuned too, although unused since the children had gone, as neither of us could play it. Our son and daughter had keyboards, and didn't want a piano: it was very bulky, enormously heavy, and couldn't do backing percussion or even record what you played. No-one else in the family needed it. We contacted a shop to sell it, but they said it was too old. We got in touch with a man who places pianos in railway stations and so on, but he said he already had over thirty on his waiting list. We had to face the sad fact that nobody wants an old piano, no matter how good it sounds.

The reason the instrument was so heavy is that, surrounded by lots of wood, of a dense and solid sort no longer used for making things, was a piece of cast iron, to which all the strings were attached, weighing about 35 stone! So I phoned a couple of scrap merchants. Surely they would be attracted by the iron. Alas no, maybe if we had a ton of scrap iron they would have come, but for one item it simply wasn't worth turning up in a lorry to collect it. And then they'd have the time and expense of getting the iron out the middle of the piano. So, with much regret, we came to a fateful decision: we would dismantle it, and dispose of the pieces as opportunity offered.

The job took several days. Neither of us being young, we couldn't just whack it to pieces with a sledgehammer. We couldn't even get it out of the dining room, it was so heavy. And also, being of a curious disposition, it would be an education to us to dismantle it in an orderly manner: a final sign of appreciation and respect. The boards at the front and the piece of cloth at the back came off easily. Now the keys could be lifted out and conveyed in a black bag to the dustbin.

Likewise the hammer actions, each one beautifully made from small wooden parts. Wire-cutters and heavy gloves dealt with the strings, and a device from eBay for 8.99 removed the tuning pegs, a tedious but in the end satisfying task. Now all that remained was the cast iron and a lot of heavy wood, held together with gigantic screws, and several horses worth of glue. Little by little, using my electric saw, I removed about half the wood. Finally we paid some men to come and take the corpse away. They managed to get it out of the front door and pushed it down onto its back on the drive. Then the sledgehammer came into play. Even after further destruction the thing was too heavy to lift onto their truck, and reinforcements had to be called. Finally we waved goodbye to the sad relic that had once been a proud and respected instrument, the joy of many families down the years, as it lay amongst the wreckage of 1970s sofas and bathrooms, on the back of the junk man's lorry.

I must admit, we were tired that night, and a bottle of fine Chilean red wine, along with a lamb shank each (straight from the microwave), roast potatoes and broccoli, soon finished us off.

I woke up in the middle of the night. It was the wine of course, it always does that. But there was something odd. I could hear, not very loudly, but distinctly, a piano being played. Beethoven's *Für Elise*. But it was coming from downstairs! Anne's breathing was quite steady. I gave her little shake, but she just turned over and slept on. I slipped out of bed, groped for my dressing gown, and crept out of the room, closing the door carefully behind me. Now the music was louder. I felt my way down the stairs and reached the dining room door. Now there could be no doubt, that's where the music was coming from. The unmistakeable sound of our old piano. I stood still, and listened, afraid to move on. What would I find in the room?

The piece came to an end, and I felt as if I'd been released from a spell. I shook myself. Anne must have left a CD in the player. I opened the door. The lamp on the low shelf was on, though its light was dim, but in the armchair by it I could see someone sitting. He rose as I came in. A man of medium height and perhaps not yet fifty years of age, with a well-groomed beard and moustache, dressed in a green smoking jacket, with brown trousers and leather slippers on his feet. An odd appearance for a burglar.

"*Bonjour, Monsieur* Henryson. I am so pleased to meet you. My name is Aristide Claudel." He stretched out his hand, then pulled it back. "*Eh bien*, what am I thinking? This is of course not permitted."

I must have just stared at him dumbly, for he gestured to the other chair. "Please, do sit down. I have much to tell you. But first, I must express my sincerest thanks to you. You, and your beautiful wife, are the agents of my liberation."

"I heard the music," was all I could manage.

"But of course, that was my favourite piece, you know. I was actually playing it when...But I must explain. You have just destroyed your old piano."

"Yes. We couldn't find anyone who..."

"*Exactement*!" he cried. "And that was my salvation, my soul's release from a century of imprisonment."

"I don't understand."

"Please, do not worry. I will explain all." He produced from behind the chair a bottle of brandy and two small glasses. Placing one on the shelf next to me, he filled it and did the same for himself. He glanced at the bottle. "A hundred and twenty years old. It should be very good indeed. *A votre santé*, Monsieur Henryson." He raised his glass and took a sip. I did likewise. It did indeed taste good. The warmth of the spirit filled me, and relaxed me.

"I must admit," I said, "I have no idea what is going on here, and whether I'm even dreaming this. But I don't think you mean me any harm and I'd like to know why you're here. It's clearly to do with our piano."

"*Exactement*," he said again, this time with less gusto and more reassurance. "I tell you all. This piano, that is now no more, it was my own, you know, it sat in the parlour of our house in the Rue de Martinique, number 34. I remember the day it came, straight from the workshop of Monsieur Érard. It came on a cart and required four men to bring it into the house. Then of course we must bring the tuner after a few days, after the piano has acclimatised. Then we could enjoy it. I played it most. My wife, Josephine, she was not so good in her playing but good enough. And we could play the duets also. Ah, those were the days." He paused to take another sip of brandy.

"Ah, but all was not so good, you see. For my wife, she had taken a lover, a cabinet maker by the name of Jacques Mireau, and they planned for my demise. They hatched a clever plan. I must go to Lyon for a few days. I am, you see, a dealer in rare and valuable objects, and I was hoping to purchase the collection of an old gentleman who had died. While I was away, Mireau came to the house, crawled under the parlour floor, placed props under the floorboards on which the piano sat, and partially sawed through the boards under the front castors. He attached ropes to the props, and led the ropes through to the cupboard under the staircase. Here he waited for my return.

"I came back on the evening train from Lyon and took a cab to the house. I was in a good mood, as my business had gone well. My wife – oh perfidious creature – welcomed me with a warm embrace and brought me a glass of brandy. The maid had left out some cold meats and bread before going home, so I was able to have a little supper. After a couple of glasses I felt more relaxed, and when Josephine suggested I play a few familiar melodies on the piano I was more than happy to oblige. I played two or three pieces, and then came to *Für Elise*. As I started to play it, Josephine excused herself, and left the room humming the tune along with my playing. At that moment, the world felt good.

"And then, all of a sudden, the piano lurched towards me. Sat on the stool with both legs on the pedals, I could not escape. The huge weight fell upon me, crushing my legs, pelvis and chest, and breaking my back as it continued its downward path, crushing the stool along with me. The only positive aspect of this hateful deed – for I know now who was responsible – was that I did not suffer long. My life was extinguished within seconds, and my soul set free to rise to the heavenly pastures.

"And now here is most strange part of the story, for the

piano, which it seems had relished and warmed to my playing so much, could not let my soul depart. But rather, it drew my poor essence within itself before it could float free, so that I was imprisoned within the very instrument which had afforded me so much pleasure in life. I called out, but what voice has a soul? I was condemned to exist within the fibres of the wood and the atoms of the cast iron, to experience at the centre of my being every single note played on that instrument since. So that a means of expressing the most beautiful music became an instrument of torture.

"Of course, after my death, my wife sold off the piano – she surely did not wish to be reminded of her foul deed. It had emerged from our encounter with only a couple of scratches and some stains, which were mostly washed away. And now my soul resounded with every clumsy child bashing out his daily exercises, and every teenage girl picking out in single notes the latest tune to take her fancy. And the lowest point was reached when the instrument was purchased for a cafe, where a gentleman with the fists of a boxer rolled out an endless programme of boogie woogie! How I suffered.

"After the Second World War, the instrument was seized by a British officer as booty of war, his excuse being that German soldiers had sat in the cafe. He organised a truck, empty now that its cargo of munitions was unloaded, and his men, with mighty effort, heaved the thing onto it. And so I reached Yorkshire. I have to say he did not play too badly. And when he died we – the piano and I – were moved to Scotland, and there the father of your wife acquired us. I felt your children's first steps on the keyboard, but thankfully they were both of a musical aptitude, and their growing skill and confidence was bearable.

"I tried to escape, of course. But with no physical being, it's very difficult. There is no muscle to place against some solid part and lever oneself away. I could make no noise. I tried to reach out to the minds of those who played me, but to no avail. And all the time the smell of sad horses assailed me, for every joint was saturated with their boiled remains. Chiefly the hoofs, of course, but who knows what else is tossed in at the glue factory.

"Until this blessed week. Of course, I heard you discussing the options, and, like you, I never believed it could turn out the way it did. But as each option was ruled out, my hopes of freedom rose. And yet still, until the very last, I could not believe you would assent to the instrument's destruction. I felt you would be swayed by the beautiful tone, or the finely polished wood, or the distinguished name of Monsieur Érard. And how my soul's heart leapt when it dawned upon me that the fateful decision was made, the doom was sealed of the house of my imprisonment.

"How I gloried in the work of destruction. I rejoiced with each twang of release as you tackled another string with the wire-cutter. I thrilled to the buzz of the electric saw as it sank into the vile woodwork. I laughed as the keys and their actions were torn out and tossed aside as rubbish. What glee I felt with every screech of protest, as the mighty carriage bolts were overpowered and drawn forth from the iron heart of the creature. What joy as the wreck was pulled forth from your front door and cast down to the earth, and as the sledgehammer destroyed the clinging remains of the woodwork, I knew that my freedom was close. And, all of a sudden, as the four strong young men heaved the still weighty remnant onto their truck, I felt the air around me, the blessed air. Oh, *mon ami*, *mon cher ami*, I cannot convey to you the supreme ecstasy of that moment. Can you imagine, after more than a hundred years, my soul was at last released. I laughed, I danced, I sang, although none saw or heard, for I was but air myself, a substance ethereal.

"And so I've came here this evening to express my thanks to you, for bringing my bondage to a close. You may feel you have lost a fine instrument, but I pray, have no feelings of guilt on this account. Instead rejoice, that you set free a soul long confined within it." As he smiled at me a tear ran down his cheek. He raised his glass again. "Monsieur Henryson, I thank you from the bottom of my heart."

I raised mine too, and drank. In truth, I was finding it hard to take in what he'd been telling me. The absurd question pushed its way into my head, where did the bottle and glasses come from? I held the glass in my hand, felt the liquor in my mouth. He seemed to read my thoughts.

"These are minor details, *mon ami*, all things are possible in this situation. By the way, I believe you earn a living by translating?"

"Yes, mainly from French."

"*Naturellement.* Your accent, by the way, is very good. I will see how I may help you."

"But don't you have to, you know, pass on to..."

"Ah yes, and I look forward to whatever door opens to me. But I have a little respite first, which I mean to enjoy."

With that he stood up. "*Bien*, now I must be elsewhere, and so, Monsieur, I bid you farewell. Please, do not stand yourself. There is no need to show me to the front door. I think you should have another glass of brandy. Please keep the bottle. Au revoir!" With that he turned and moved silently, and remarkably quickly, through the open doorway at the rear of the room, leading into the kitchen.

It must have been a few moments before I recovered my senses. I jumped up, ran through to the kitchen, and flicked the light on. But, of course, he was gone. And now I felt very tired, and slightly woozy. I thought that I must tell Anne at once, but when I reached the bedroom, I was so tired I merely crawled into bed and fell at once asleep.

When I woke up the next morning, I thought I must have been dreaming, and told Anne the story. She nodded. "You know, darling, I always felt there was something about that piano. Something more. And I know this sounds daft, but when they heaved the remains of it onto the truck, I felt a huge sense of relief. Maybe there was more to it all. And your dream is part of that." And downstairs, in the dining room, on the low shelf by the two chairs, stood two small glasses and a bottle of very old brandy.

You may think that's the end of the story, but there is one further scene to tell. A couple of weeks later I had occasion to travel into Glasgow for a meeting with a client. My train came into the low level platform at Glasgow Central, and, as I came up out of the escalator onto the ground level, I heard the distant sound of a piano, playing *Für Elise*. I hurried down to the main concourse, for I knew there was a piano there.

As I got closer, I could see the upright piano but not the player. On top of the piano sat a grey Homburg hat on a folded newspaper. As the piece finished, I was still traversing a party of Japanese tourists wheeling much luggage. The pianist stood up, and I recognised Monsieur Claudel. He looked at me, and smiled. He was wearing a long black coat of a very old-fashioned style. He put the hat on his head, then waved the folded paper at me and put it back down. At that moment a suitcase ran over my feet, and I had to acknowledge the apologies of the small and wizened old gentleman responsible. When I was able to look back to the piano, Claudel was gone.

I reached the piano in a few moments. All that remained of my night visitor was the newspaper. I picked it up, and felt immediately that there was something else inside. It was a faded envelope, about A5 in size, sealed with a blob of red wax, and containing the inscription, in flowing handwriting, the ink much faded: 'M. Aristide Claudel.' I could feel that it contained several sheets of paper. I put it in my rucksack – it could wait until I was home. I sat on a nearby bench and looked more closely at the newspaper. It was a copy of *Paris Soir* dated 14th July 1912. Not as yellowed by age as I would have expected.

I scanned the front page, and my gaze was arrested by a headline at the bottom right hand corner, which I translate as 'Final Notes of the Piano Murderers.' The piece announced that Jacques Mireau and Josephine Claudel had, that morning at 7 a.m., been executed by the guillotine for the murder of Claudel's husband Aristide. It described how, one day in April, Mireau, hidden in a cupboard in Claudel's house, and with the connivance of his wife, had cleverly contrived a piano to fall upon the unfortunate M. Claudel, crushing him instantly to death. At first the collapse of the floorboard beneath part of the piano had been ascribed to rot or weakness in the wood; however, careful examination by a sharp-eyed detective had revealed the boards to have been sawn through, and a few days later the pair were apprehended at the Gare de Lyon whilst trying to flee the city. Mme Claudel soon confessed, blaming Mireau for the conception and execution of the whole scheme, whilst Mireau claimed he had been hired by Mme. Claudel to kill her husband. The jury was not long in declaring the pair guilty, and the judge pronounced the dread sentence, carried out that very morning.

Back home that afternoon, in the presence of my wife, I opened the envelope. It contained a wad of thin paper, each sheet covered on both sides with closely packed writing in the same flowing hand as on the envelope. On top was a scrap of paper, on which was written, in the same hand, and I again translate, 'To my esteemed friend Aristide Claudel, I enclose my final work.'

It was signed 'Jules Verne' and dated 17 January 1905. I had in my possession an autograph copy of an unpublished work of the famous author. It was entitled *The Time Traveller*. You can imagine that my annotated edition in the original French, and my translation into English, set my finances on a very healthy course. However, Anne and I decided we would still downsize, and now we have a comfortable bungalow on the Ayrshire coast, looking across to the mountains of Arran. Pride of place on our dining table is an empty brandy bottle, a very old one, into whose neck we have placed a candle.

Epilogue

The Critical Reader

In one of the smaller tents of the Edinburgh Book Festival, crime writer Kyle McClaver has given his talk and is signing copies of his latest book, *Death from Beyond*, number nineteen in the Inspector Platt series. He signs each book with a bored squiggle, without a glance at the purchaser. He licks his lips, imagines a cool gin and tonic at the refreshment tent.

The final reader looms, but no book slides under his pen. He glances up, sees a bushy beard and moustache, dark glasses, pork-pie hat. Some weirdos come to these events. Still, if they buy the books…

The man bends down, speaks quietly into Kyle's ear. "Sorry, I've no book to sign, Kyle. I've read it already. It's shite. But you knew that already. A bogus medium drapes his victims in fake ectoplasm. That might have worked in 1905. Maybe. Let's face it, Kyle, you've run out of ideas. It's time Inspector Platt retired."

The knife thrust through Kyle's carotid artery and into his windpipe is quick, firm, and clean. With an expert twist it's removed, and Kyle chokes on his own blood. The man talks soothingly to Kyle as the writer's head sinks onto the table-top. Then he straightens up, slipping the knife into his canvas shopping bag.

He reaches the tent door. The student on duty, immersed in her iPhone, sees him with a start, hurriedly pockets the phone, opens the door. He adopts his best French: "*Merci, ma'amoiselle. Un ééement trè intéessant. Mais, je pense*, er, I think Monsieur McClaver is not well. Perhaps you can help him." He passes through the door and she closes it, then heads over to the recumbent form of the writer. Only when she sees the blood does she grope for her phone again.

Meanwhile, in the narrow space between two tents, the man divests himself of the facial hair, the glasses and the hat, drops them into the bag. He takes off and adds to them his linen jacket; after all, it's a warm day. As he leaves the festival precinct, and heads for Princes Street, an ambulance passes, screeching to a halt by the ornate festival gateway.

He gets his bus on the bridge over Waverley Station, and sits upstairs, on the left. As the bus turns onto Dalkeith Road and passes the Commonwealth Pool, he remembers the volume he bought earlier at the bookshop tent, and takes it out. *Tales Murderous and Mysterious.* Well, he thinks, this one better be good.

About the Author
Allan Martin

Allan Martin worked as a teacher, teacher-trainer and university lecturer. He turned to writing fiction after taking early retirement, and has never looked back. His first novel, *The Peat Dead*, was shortlisted for the inaugural McIlvanney Debut Prize in 2019.

In addition to the Angus Blue series, he writes crime novels set in 1930s Estonia, and writes short stories for *iScot* magazine and book reviews for *Aspects of History*.

He has also translated from Estonian a closed-room mystery, *The Oracle*, originally published in 1937. *The Peat Dead* was published in Estonian by Eesti Raamat in 2021, as *Turbasurnud*.

Allan lives just north of Glasgow with his wife Vivien (also a writer). They regularly visit the Highlands and Islands, as well as Germany and Estonia.

The Peat Dead
Allan Martin

Shortlisted for the 2019 Bloody Scotland McIlvanney Debut Scottish Crime Prize.

ISBN: 978-1-910946-55-8 (Kindle)
ISBN: 978-1-910946-54-1 (Paperback)

On the Scottish Hebridean Island of Islay, five corpses are dug up by a peat-cutter. All of them have been shot in the back of the head, execution style.

Sent across from the mainland to investigate, Inspector Angus Blue and his team slowly piece together the little evidence they have, and discover the men were killed on a wartime base, over 70 years ago.

But there are still secrets worth protecting, and even killing for. Who can Inspector Blue trust?

"A mystery so redolent of its island setting that you practically smell the peat and whisky on the pages." – Douglas Skelton"

This atmospheric crime novel set on Islay gripped me from the start. A book that shows decades-old crimes cast long shadows." – Sarah Ward

The Dead of Jura
Allan Martin
ISBN: 978-1-910946-55-8 (Kindle)
ISBN: 978-1-910946-68-8 (Paperback)

Jura: where the rich and the powerful come to play, away from the prying eyes of the press.

But when there is an assassination attempt on a Cabinet Minister while he's on his island estate, questions must be asked, and Inspector Angus Blue and his team return to the Hebrides to investigate.

Deemed a matter of 'National Security' by London, local protocols are overruled, and Special Branch officers are sent to hunt down the assassin. By the time Inspector Blue and his team arrive the estate staff have been scared into silence, and the crime scene has been disturbed.

His investigation hampered at every turn, Inspector Blue must discover what Special Branch are hiding – and who they are protecting.

The Dead of Jura is the second novel in the Inspector Angus Blue Series.

"Subtle, complex and intense as a fine island malt."
Olga Wojtas

"A 'must read' for fans of Scottish crime fiction"
Marion Todd

The Dead of Appin
Allan Martin
ISBN: 978-1-910946-83-1 (Kindle)
ISBN: 978-1-910946-82-4 (Paperback)

Just outside Oban, within sight of the Connel Bridge, there's a burnt out car containing the charred remains of a human body. A woman is missing – but is the body hers?

In a high stakes game of business and politics, what secret does the bustling port of Oban hide that is worth killing for?

The Dead of Appin is the third book in the Inspector Blue series.

'Intricate and exciting. Scottish crime fiction at its best. – Marion Todd

'The Dead of Appin is another cracking installment in the Angus Blue series, embark on whisky flavoured adventures in the west Highlands as Blue is drawn into a dangerous world of intrigue and corruption. Addictive from page one!' – G. R. Halliday

'A complex mystery starring the unforgettable Angus Blue as he explores political corruption and grisly murders in the Scottish highlands. And he cooks too! Don't miss it.' – Emma Christie

In The Shadow Of The Hill
Helen Forbes

ISBN: 978-0-9929768-1-1 (eBook)
ISBN: 978-0-9929768-0-4 (Paperback)

An elderly woman is found battered to death in the common stairwell of an Inverness block of flats.

Detective Sergeant Joe Galbraith starts what seems like one more depressing investigation of the untimely death of a poor unfortunate who was in the wrong place, at the wrong time.

As the investigation spreads across Scotland it reaches into a past that Joe has tried to forget, and takes him back to the Hebridean island of Harris, where he spent his childhood.

Among the mountains and the stunning landscape of religiously conservative Harris, in the shadow of Ceapabhal, long buried events and a tragic story are slowly uncovered, and the investigation takes on an altogether more sinister aspect.

In The Shadow Of The Hill skilfully captures the intricacies and malevolence of the underbelly of Highland and Island life, bringing tragedy and vengeance to the magical beauty of the Outer Hebrides.

'…our first real home-grown sample of modern Highland noir'
– Roger Hutchinson; West Highland Free Press

Madness Lies
Helen Forbes

ISBN: 978-1-910946-31-2 (Kindle)
ISBN: 978-1-910946-30-5 (Paperback)

When an Inverness Councillor is murdered in broad daylight in the middle of town, Detective Sergeant Joe Galbraith sees a familiar figure running from the scene.

According to everyone who knows him, the Councillor had no enemies, but someone clearly wanted him dead.

The victim's high profile means the police want a quick resolution to the case, but no one seems to know anything. Or if they do, they're not prepared to say.

This second novel of Highland Noir from Helen Forbes continues the series with a crime thriller that moves between Inverness, North Uist and London, reaching a terrifying denouement at the notorious Black Rock Gorge.

'You would expect Helen Forbes to write well of an exile's experience of Sollas, Vallay and west side of North Uist, and she does. She evokes the machair, the changing sky and sea, the flowers, birds and waving grass, the dunes, the people and above all the peace.' – Roger Hutchinson; West Highland Free Press

The Birds That Never Flew
Margot McCuaig

Longlisted for the Polari First Book Prize 2014

ISBN: 978-0-9575689-3-8 (Kindle)
ISBN: 978-0-9929768-4-2 (Paperback)

'Have you got a light hen? I'm totally gaspin.'

Battered and bruised, Elizabeth has taken her daughter and left her abusive husband Patrick. Again. In the bleak and impersonal Glasgow housing office Elizabeth meets the provocatively intriguing drug addict Sadie, who is desperate to get her own life back on track.

The two women forge a fierce and interdependent relationship as they try to rebuild their shattered lives, but despite their bold, and sometimes illegal attempts it seems impossible to escape from the abuse they have always known, and tragedy strikes.

More than a decade later Elizabeth has started to implement her perfect revenge - until a surreal Glaswegian Virgin Mary steps in with imperfect timing and a less than divine attitude to stick a spoke in the wheel of retribution.

Tragic, darkly funny and irreverent, The Birds That Never Flew is a new and vibrant voice in Scottish literature.

"Not Scandinavian but dark, beautiful and moving, I wholeheartedly recommend" – scanoir.co.uk

The Deaths on the Black Rock
BRM Stewart

ISBN: 978-1-910946-47-3 (Kindle)
ISBN: 978-1-910946-46-6 (Paperback)

It's been a year since Rima Khalaf died in a fall from the Black Rock, deemed to be a tragic accident by the police.

But her grieving parents are dissatisfied with the police investigation, so DS Amanda Pitt is sent north from Glasgow to the small town of Clachdubh to re-examine the case.

Despite the suspicions of the distraught parents, all the circumstances seem to confirm Rima's death was indeed a tragic accident, until another woman is also found dead in the town.

Frustrated by the lack of any real evidence, DS Pitt pushes the limits of legality in her quest for the truth.

Stewart writes with a gritty intensity that places the reader in intimate contact with the darker side of society, in a way that forces you to empathise with the uncomfortable idea that sometimes the end justifies the means for those who are supposed to uphold the law.

Toxic
Jackie McLean

Shortlisted for the Yeovil Book Prize 2011

ISBN: 978-0-9575689-8-3 (eBook)
ISBN: 978-0-9575689-9-0 (Paperback)

The recklessly brilliant DI Donna Davenport, struggling to hide a secret from police colleagues and get over the break-up with her partner, has been suspended from duty for a fiery and inappropriate outburst to the press.

DI Evanton, an old-fashioned, hard-living misogynistic copper has been newly demoted for thumping a suspect, and transferred to Dundee with a final warning ringing in his ears and a reputation that precedes him.

And in the peaceful, rolling Tayside farmland a deadly store of MIC, the toxin that devastated Bhopal, is being illegally stored by a criminal gang smuggling the valuable substance necessary for making cheap pesticides.

An anonymous tip-off starts a desperate search for the MIC that is complicated by the uneasy partnership between Davenport and Evanton and their growing mistrust of each others actions.

Compelling and authentic, Toxic is a tense and fast paced crime thriller.

'...a humdinger of a plot that is as realistic as it is frightening'
– crimefictionlover.com

Shadows
Jackie McLean

ISBN: 978-1-910946-29-9 (Kindle)
ISBN: 978-1-910946-28-2 (Paperback)

When DI Donna Davenport is called out to investigate a body washed up on Arbroath beach, it looks like a routine murder inquiry. But then the enquiry takes on a more sinister form.

There are similarities with a previous murder, and now a woman connected to them both has also gone missing. For Donna, this is becoming personal, and with the added pressure of feeling watched at every turn, she is convinced that Jonas Evanton has returned to seek his revenge on her for his downfall.

Fearing they may be looking for a serial killer, Donna and her new team are taken in a horrifying and unexpected direction. Because it's not a serial killer - it's worse.

Moving from Dundee to the south coast of Turkey and the Syrian border, this is a fast paced novel about those who live their lives in the shadows, and those who exploit them.

"With sensitivity and honesty, Jackie has written a thriller that will shock and grip the reader in equal measure."

Run
Jackie McLean

ISBN: 978-1-910946-65-7 (Kindle)
ISBN: 978-1-910946-64-0 (Paperback)

RUN THE GAUNTLET

DI Donna Davenport and her team are under pressure.

With the hunt on for the country's most notorious cop killer, and an ongoing complex international investigation, the murder of a local thug during a football match is the last thing the police need.

But as more incidents overload the police, and fear brings vigilante mobs onto the streets, suspicion grows that the mayhem is being orchestrated.

CUT AND RUN

One man can make it stop. With the city heading towards chaos and disaster Donna prepares to abandon caution and the rules, even if it means she is ostracised by her own team.

"A superbly plotted and gripping police procedural that will leave you breathless. McLean has excelled herself with Run" – Tana Collins